Standish O'Grady

Lost on Du-Corrig

or 'Twixt earth and Ocean

Standish O'Grady

Lost on Du-Corrig
or 'Twixt earth and Ocean

ISBN/EAN: 9783337034160

Printed in Europe, USA, Canada, Australia, Japan

Cover: Foto ©Andreas Hilbeck / pixelio.de

More available books at **www.hansebooks.com**

"TAKING MY CLUE WITH ME, I DIVED" (*p.* 198).

OR

TWIXT EARTH AND OCEAN

BY

STANDISH O'GRADY

AUTHOR OF "FINN AND HIS COMPANIONS," "THE BOG OF STARS,
"THE STORY OF IRELAND," ETC.

CASSELL AND COMPANY LIMITED
LONDON PARIS & MELBOURNE
1894

PREFACE.

I HAD at first intended to tell this story myself. With that intention I wrote to each of the four brothers who separately or together figured in the singular events hereafter described, requesting of them more exact information than I already possessed. They replied not only at such length, but with such unexpectedly vivid realism, that their various narratives, in spite of some literary shortcomings, seemed to me to need only a little editorial revision to fit them for publication. I perceived that I would more prudently play the part of editor than of original author. Accordingly, I decided to let the brothers Freeman tell their own story. When their narratives overlapped I simply used the scissors. When too minute or too wandering I struck my pen through the redundancies, or what appeared to me to be such, endeavouring to secure a little more brevity and conciseness. Some slight discrepancies, chiefly in the matter of dates, I was enabled to correct from an old volume of the *Saunders Newsletter*. It was there that I first became acquainted with the details of the singular disappearance of John Freeman, though long before the story was familiar to me in its more general features. By the kindness of the Authorities of Dublin Castle I was permitted to inspect and take copies of the official reports sent in by the Police Sub-Inspector of the district. Along with these reports I found tied up in the same bundle a number of letters of a more private character written by the same Police Officer and addressed to the same superior to whom were forwarded the official reports. These two persons—viz., the local Sub-Inspector of Constabulary, who wrote the reports and letters, and the permanent official in the Castle to whom they were addressed—seem to have been intimate friends. On the top of the bundle I found a single sheet with the following endorsement :—

"It has occurred to me that sooner or later

some person will undertake to write out and publish in all its details the whole story of the mysterious and unaccountable disappearance of John Freeman, a story which illustrates again for the thousandth time the old adage that truth is stranger than fiction. I have, therefore, decided to deposit here, along with the official reports forwarded to me by Mr. Samuel Watkins, the private letters which, simultaneously with the official, or from time to time, he may have written to me dealing with the catastrophe. In these private letters the inquirer, whoever he may be, and whenever he comes along this way making his searches, will meet with a large variety of local and personal details very suitable for his purpose, but for obvious reasons unfit to form part of Mr. Watkins' official reports.

"HENRY VIGORS."

Mr. Watkins, of whose letters I have made a copious use, is dead; so is Mr. Vigors. These letters are very interesting not only as exhibiting the attitude of an intelligent Constabulary

A *

officer towards the main incident and its developments, but also on account of the light which they throw upon the Freeman family. Then the letters of a person, written at the time of the occurrence of the tragedy, or whatever it may be called, will, I think, help the reader to picture the events and characters with more vividness. The letters of Mr. Watkins I have treated in the same manner as the narratives of the brothers. In fact, I have done little more than cross the t's and pip the i's of the various persons whom I allow here to relate the history of the singular disappearance and singular adventures of John Freeman.

I beg publicly to thank the brothers not only for responding so promptly to my appeal, but for their permission to publish, with such alterations as I might see fit to make, what they never intended should come before the public eye in the form in which it left their pens. I may add that the warm mutual affection of the brothers, the primitive character of the neighbourhood, and the simplicity of the home life of the Freeman family, which are pleasantly and naturally suggested rather than elaborately described in their various communications, are such as I myself, though a seasoned litterateur, felt convinced that I could not reproduce with anything like the freshness and vividness of their unlaboured composition. Of the four brothers who were concerned in the events described, Samuel, the third, hereinafter spoken of invariably as Sam, is the only one whose narrative I have not used, but for no other reason than that it is quite overlapped by those of the rest. John Freeman, the hero of the story, is the lad who was lost; Edward Freeman is the discoverer of the lost one. The part played by Charles, the youngest, and also some singular experiences of the hero, are very curious, and suggest interesting questions in psychology. I am happy to state that all four, though now scattered far and wide over the earth's surface, are doing well, and all, except the youngest, are married men and fathers of families. Editor.

CONTENTS.

LIST OF ILLUSTRATIONS.

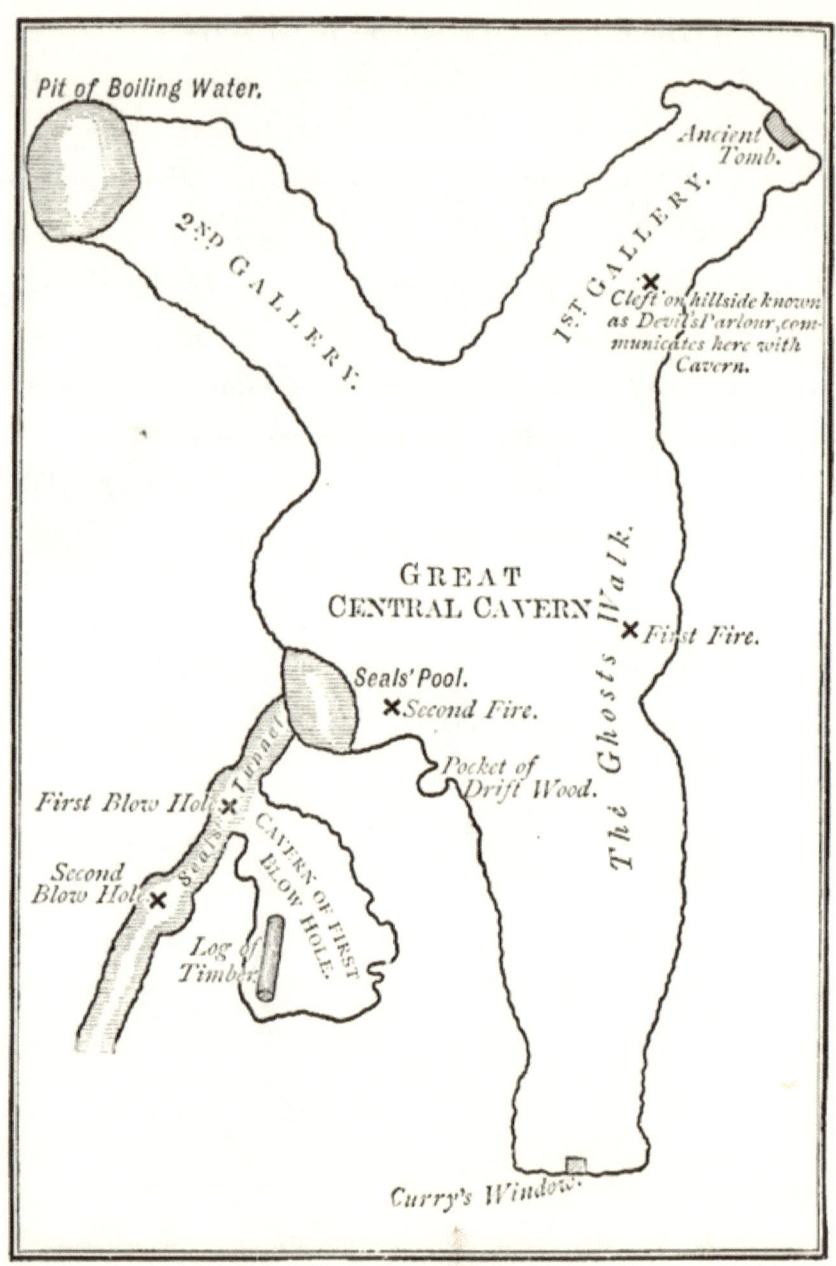

Pit of Boiling Water.

Ancient Tomb.

2ND GALLERY.

1ST GALLERY.

×
Cleft on hillside known
as Devil's Parlour, com-
municates here with
Cavern.

GREAT
CENTRAL CAVERN

The Ghosts Walk.

× First Fire.

Seals' Pool.
× Second Fire.

First Blow Hole
× Seals' Tunnel

Second
Blow Hole ×

CAVERN OF FIRST
BLOW HOLE.

Pocket of
Drift Wood.

Log of
Timber

Curry's Window.

PLAN OF THE CAVERN.

LOST ON DU-CORRIG.

CHAPTER I.

CHARLES FREEMAN'S NARRATIVE.—MY BROTHER
GOES TO DU-CORRIG.

IN the month of July, 1854, my eldest brother,
John Freeman, suddenly and most unaccountably was taken from us. One fine afternoon,
being in good health and spirits, he went
fishing and never returned. At lunch he
was very pleasant and even jocose, making us
youngsters laugh so immoderately that my
father was at last obliged to interfere, and one
of my brothers was sent out of the room in
disgrace.

All the events of that terrible day are im-
printed on my mind with the clearness of
visuality. I can still see the funny faces with
which, when my father was not looking, he
threw us into uncontrollable laughing fits. He

B

had but just returned from Trinity College for
the summer vacation, and was full of all sorts
of joyous plans and projects for spending a good
time at home. Poor fellow! he little knew
what this vacation had in store for him.

For a boy like my brother, and, indeed, for
all of us, few rural neighbourhoods could have
been more delightful than ours. There were
mountain streams abounding with trout, streams
which needed only a night's rain, sometimes
merely a heavy shower, to supply good fishing.
When the streams were not flooded he often
brought home a good basket of brown trout
and white, taken in the pools and holes with a
mere shrimping-net which he made himself. It
was something like a large and long-handled
landing-net.

There were good trout lakes, too, in the
mountains. Of sea-fishing, both from boats
and from the rock, he was very fond; he was
at the latter sport, viz., fishing for conor* from

---

* A dull-yellow fish, very scaly, not welcome to epicures,
and affording poor sport.—ED.

a rock, when he so mysteriously disappeared.
The Atlantic, beating against a very wild and
almost iron-bound coast, lay less than a mile
from our home. My father, a clergyman of the
Church of Ireland, before the world suspected it
to be a "upas tree," was incumbent of a very
large parish, in fact three parishes rolled into
one, which extended many miles along the sea-
coast and far into the interior. There were no
resident gentry, and there was no preservation
of game.

No one but my brother had a gun in all the
country-side, so that the shooting was all ours,
and there was shooting in summer as well as in
winter, for in summer we shot curlews, cave-
pigeons, rabbits, and hares. Puss abounded in
this region, and as there were no harriers and
no greyhounds, Jack was, in fact, not only a
great sportsman, but the only sportsman in the
county. Enemies he had none, so that his mysterious disappearance could not be ascribed to
any personal malignity. All the country people
were fond of him, and, I think, proud of

him. They were always bringing him
news of the "whereabouts" of otters, badgers,
coveys of partridge, and so forth, and would
run across the fields, leaving their work,
to learn the contents of his bag, or would
shout from afar, when they saw him returning
with rod or gun, "Well, Master John, what
luck?"

No, we never suspected for a moment, not
until months after his disappearance, that he had
been made away with by an enemy or had met
with any foul play. And yet, in broad daylight,
less than a mile from the Rectory, my brother
suddenly disappeared, vanished as utterly as if
he had been sucked down into the bowels of the
earth, or drawn up into the sky.

The day was the 10th of July, a singularly
fine day even for that time of the year. It was
the day after his return from college, and he
was quite running over with spirits. When I
awoke early that morning I heard him whistling
outside the windows on the lawn. The air was
"Vilikins and his Dinah," a song much in vogue

at the time. He always came home with a new tune, and never seemed to tire of it till he got another. When I looked out he was walking to and fro on the lawn, taking the twist out of a new fishing-line. He had fastened one end of it to a little holly-tree on the lawn, and was diligently engaged in taking out the twist, which, indeed, is a tedious process.

During the forenoon and on till dinner-time he seemed keenly and happily absorbed in similar avocations, viz., getting his fishing-gear into order. We youngsters were confined to the schoolroom all that time, which we considered unfair, inasmuch as it was Jack's first day at home, but we could hear him bustling about the place and everlastingly whistling " Vilikins and his Dinah." Once we heard an awful screaming of geese in the rear regions. We knew perfectly well the cause of it. Jack was pursuing them and plucking out their wing feathers in order to tie pollock-flies.

A little after noon he came into the school-room and asked the tutor, Mr. Humphreys, to let me go to the village to buy him some wire. He gave me a penny for the wire and a penny for myself. In those days I considered a penny a handsome tip. He wanted the wire to make line-eyes for his big rod, that which he used for sea-fishing. He also bade me call at the shoe-maker's to get a piece of wax. I mention all this because on his disappearance some foolish people said that he had " run away," a suppos-ition which no member of the family harboured for a single instant. He was, in fact, brimful of sporting intentions.

At three we dined, when, as I have described, he made those funny faces and set us all on the roar. When dinner was over and we ran out of the room, there was a boy at the hall door with a box of bait in his hand, consisting partly of cockles and partly of what we used to call lug-worms. They are dug up in the mud of the sea-shore when the tide is out. This boy had been digging bait for Jack all the morning. He asked Jack to let him go with him to Du-Corrig, and Jack refused.

" Where are you going, Jack ? " said my second brother, Ned.

" To Du-Corrig for conor," he said ; "and let none of you follow me as you value your lives."

Young as I was, by a certain sympathy, or I know not what, I saw why he wished to be alone. It was to indulge in his transports and talk and sing, and do what he pleased, and so let off his animal spirits and delight at being home again, without witnesses. I generally knew and felt what was passing in his mind. Indeed, I was very much attached to him, though he took hardly any notice of me. I was greatly pleased this day because he had selected me to go for the wire and wax.

" I shall slay the wily conor, Ned," he went on, "till the sun is just *that high* above the western main.

Sing tooral-al-ooral-al-ooral-al-lee,

and then, up with the white feather! and in with pollock and crohogues! till Apollo is half-

way to the North in his silver boat, and black
night invests the sea.

> For a cup of cold pison it lay by her side,
> And the billet-doux said 'twas by pison she died.
> *Sing tooral-al-ooral-al-ooral-al-lee."*

etc., etc.

Off he marched down the avenue with his
little box of bait in his left hand, and his rod on
his right shoulder, crunching the gravel noisily,
for he was a large and stout lad. The two dogs
followed close at his heels with their tails down,
for they feared that they would be turned back.
So they were, at the gate, and when they still
showed signs of following he stooped down and
flung stones towards them. Shortly afterwards
I heard him shout " Ter."

" Sir? " answered a voice from a neighbour-
ing field.

" Come to Du-Corrig an hour after sunset to
bring home the fish."

"I will, sir," answered the voice.

Then I heard more faintly in the distance
the plaintive notes of " Vilikins and his Dinah "

—an odious song, by the way. So my brother Jack left home that 10th of July, 1854, and was not seen again. As will be quite evident, he could have no intention whatever of " running away," and yet that was the explanation of his disappearance which was favoured by all the Solomons.

CHAPTER II.

AND DOES NOT RETURN.

I KNOW not why, but I had an uneasy feeling about Jack all that day, and it increased after he had left the Rectory for Du-Corrig. For some time this uneasy feeling took no precise shape, but later on I began to picture to myself a "tidal wave" sweeping him off the rock, and, having a lively imagination, saw the imaginary scene clearly, and Jack struggling for his life in the water. In the previous summer three tenants of ours in a different part of the country, all fathers of families, had been so swept off the rocks while fishing conor and drowned.

Though I reminded myself that Jack was a splendid swimmer and diver, and could do any-thing in the water, I failed to get rid of the vague sense of coming calamity of which I was conscious all day, and which became greater and greater as the sun set and darkness came on.

" Might not Jack be attacked by cramp," I thought, " when in the water ? "

True he never had had a cramp, nor did I know of anyone who was ever assailed in that way, but I had heard a great deal about the cramp.

I was sent to bed early, for I was only eight years old, but I could not sleep. I kept listening for the barking of the dogs. In the previous summer that was to me the usual sign that Jack had returned safe from fishing. It was now long after dark. My two elder brothers, Ned and Sam, came into the room with a lamp. We three slept in the same room, Ned and Sam in one large bed, I in a little timber bedstead with high sides, over which I had to climb when getting in and out.

Ned put the lamp on the table opposite the looking-glass and leaned over it. He took a pin from his coat and began to push up the wick. It was a primitive little lamp : I have not seen such since I was a boy. There was usually a fat red head on the top of the wick,

which had to be snuffed just as we used to snuff
the candles.

"Jack is out late to-night," he said; "I
hope nothing has happened him."

"What could happen him?" said Sam, who
was of a more stolid character. While saying
this he undid the serpent-fastened belt which
confined his waggoner. In those days boys
wore loose white blouses gathered round the
waist by a belt; we used to call them "wag-
goners."

"I don't know," replied Ned, "but 'tis
very late. There's papa opening the hall door
and listening. How still the night is!"

"He's drowned," I cried from my truckle
bed. "The tidal wave has caught him as
it caught Cody, Phillips, and Moroney last
year."

"Hold your tongue, you little ass, and go to
sleep," answered Ned angrily, but he threw
down the window, leaned out, and listened.

There was a corn-crake craking somewhere
outside. The moon was shining; I could hear

the distant roar of the sea, where it rolled up the white strand which we called Tramore.

"This is getting bad, Sam," he said. "He's long after his time."

Sam was now in bed, but sitting up and listening with bright eyes. I heard my father moving about below stairs ceaselessly from the hall door to the parlour and back again, and talking with my mother.

"There's someone coming," said Ned. The dogs were indeed barking, but not for Jack; that I knew well. "Pooh! 'tis only old Ter."

"Well, Ter," he cried cheerfully from the window, "where are the fish? Why isn't Master John with you?"

To these questions there was no audible reply.

Ter was one of my father's labourers who worked, or rather elaborately idled, upon the extensive glebe farm which was attached to the Rectory. It will be remembered that it was Ter whom my brother told to come to Du-Corrig after sunset. Ter made no reply to Ned's questions. I heard him crunching the gravel as he walked slowly to the hall door.

"What is he saying?" I cried.

"Sh—" said Ned, with his head on one side, listening. The man was saying something to my father at the hall door.

"He says he found the bait-box on the rock, but no rod, and that Jack is not there, and that he shouted for him everywhere and got no answer. Get up, Sam; we must go search."

Sam sprang at once with a bound upon the floor and dressed in haste.

"Perhaps he left Du-Corrig," he said, "in one of the boats going out for night-fishing."

"Then why did he leave the box of bait behind him?" retorted Ned.

"Forgot it," answered Sam, dressing furiously.

The house was by this time in confusion, with servants rushing to and fro, exclamations, interrogations, and my father's voice raised.

Then I heard somewhere the sound of a horn. The country-side was being called out to search. I was alone now; Ned and Sam were far away in the night. From the window I could see many torches moving swiftly south-westwards in the direction of Du-Corrig. I heard the faintest and most distant noises, owing to the extreme stillness of the night. Fear, I suppose, too, made my hearing preter-naturally acute.

I remained at the open window a long time, till I was discovered there by my mother, shiver-ing and coughing, and was by her put back into my bed. She was in tears, though perhaps to comfort me she said, "Go to sleep, darling. Jack will be here when you wake in the morn-ing. Of course he has gone out in one of the deep-sea fishing-boats."

It was discovered, however, ere long that none of the boats which used to go out far from land, fishing haak and ling, had gone out that night, owing to stress of haymaking. At last I fell asleep. When I woke in the morning and sat up, I found my two brothers lying on their bed, outside the bed-clothes, fast asleep, but not undressed. I knew from this that Jack had not been found. I dressed and went into Jack's room. It was empty! I then went downstairs. There were voices in my father's study. The door was open; I saw my father standing and my mother sitting down, both very pale, and my mother weeping. It was still the grey dawn of the day.

My parents not having noticed me, I set out for Du-Corrig and ran all the way. The place was crowded with fishermen and country people, amongst whom were several policemen and coast-guards, in their blue jackets and white trousers. There were boats off the rock, which were being rowed slowly along. The men in them were dragging the sea-bottom here with grappling-irons. Just then a police orderly rode up on a foaming horse. He received some fresh directions from Mr. Watkins, the constabulary officer of the district, and galloped off again. Everyone, indeed, was at his wits' ends, for it was quite impossible to frame any theory of the disappearance which would square with known facts. One

boat had gone bream-fishing the previous afternoon. The people in it said that they had seen
my brother on the rock, and that he had hailed
them as they rowed past in a cheerful and
friendly manner.

That was the last seen or heard of him.
That he had been drowned no one in the neighbourhood could believe, though the coastguards,
for want of anything else to do,' were dragging
the sea-bottom. There were other boats out too
—fishermen who went miles to the east and
miles to the west, searching and at intervals
crying out, hoping against hope that there
might be some response. Presently my elder
brothers Ned and Sam came down to the rock,
and roughly bade me go home. They joined
Mr. Watkins, who questioned them for a long
time. The last hope was that in obedience to a
sudden impulse he had walked off to visit some of
our distant friends, for' a twenty or thirty mile
walk was nothing to him.

But no tidings of any kind reached us as
day followed day. No one had heard of him

c

or seen him anywhere since the bream-fishers passed him on the rock, when he hailed them as I have already described.

The series of extraordinary and marvellous experiences which had really befallen my brother will be found to re-illustrate for the thousandth time the old saying that " truth is stranger than fiction."

CHAPTER III.

" I HAVE to report a very mysterious disappearance which took place in this neighbourhood
last Wednesday, the 10th instant. The eldest
son of our rector, the Rev. Mr. Freeman, left
home in the afternoon to go fishing, and never
returned. He was seen by a boat's crew shortly
afterwards, fishing from the rock to which he
had announced that he would go for that
purpose. Its local name is Du-Corrig. For
reasons which I need not set down, I am absolutely certain that he did not run away. That
he slipped from the rock and was drowned is
also well-nigh incredible, for he was a splendid
swimmer and a remarkably athletic and spirited
young man; nor is it credible that he met with
foul play in such a spot and at such a time, for
he had nothing with him to excite cupidity.

"He was very popular, too, in the neighbourhood, and after making many secret inquiries, I do not believe that he had an enemy in the whole country-side. It is possible, no doubt, that from some other part of the country an enemy may have followed him hither, killed him unawares on the rock, and flung his body into the sea. The ground, however, has been carefully dragged, under my directions, by the coastguards of the adjoining station. They found nothing—not even his rod, which disappeared along with him.

"Subsequently I secured the services of the diver who is at work on the construction of the Coosdarig pier for the Board of Works. He came next day, with his diving apparatus and assistants, and made a careful submarine examination without discovering anything. If young Freeman was drowned here, his rod, weighted as it was by a heavy brass reel, should have been found. Altogether the case is mysterious, nor can I frame any theory which would rationally account for it. I have caused advertisements to

be inserted in all the Connaught papers, giving
a description of young Freeman."

SAMUEL WATKINS. [Private Letter.] July 18th.

MY DEAR HARRY,—You cannot imagine how much I
have been upset about this affair. John Freeman, the lost
boy—I find it hard to picture him as anything but a boy—
has been known to me intimately since he was thirteen
years of age. I can honestly say that I have never known
a finer, braver, more honourable, and more affectionate lad.
He is not exactly handsome, though he has the fiercest and
brightest eyes of glowing hazel that I ever saw, and a very
beautiful mouth; nor clever, yet, at the same time, not
deficient in intelligence. He is absolutely without vice,
though I hear that during the last college term he has
begun to smoke a little. He is the strongest and almost
the most athletic youth whom it has ever been my good
fortune to meet, large-limbed, muscular, and brimful of
health and of spirits. As a swimmer and diver I never
saw his equal. I have often seen him strip on a wild day
in December or January, and swim long distances to
recover some curlew or pigeon which he had shot. But
enough of this. Suffice it to say that not only as the
constabulary officer of this district, but as his own personal
friend, the astonishing and mysterious disappearance of
poor Freeman, under the circumstances detailed in the
official report, has been to me a most severe blow. I
have done, and am doing, my best. But every night finds
me here in my den cogitating aimlessly over this tragedy,

for the worst of it is that I am unable even to imagine a theory which will in the least square with the facts.

It is unfortunate that the Rev. Mr. Freeman and myself are not on the best of terms. I once flung out the suggestion that the days mentioned in the first chapter of Genesis were ages or long intervals of time. Some meddler told him of this, since when he has regarded me coldly and askance as a dangerous Freethinker. Moreover, I am not a very regular attendant at church. In short, our relations are cold and strained, though I like and respect him very much. John, the lost boy, is the eldest son.

The next brother is Edward—a tall, loose-jointed, black-eyed and merry stripling, far more popular than John, owing to his pleasant ways and ready speech, greatly devoted to flute-playing and performances on the cornet-à-piston, a magnificent leaper and swimmer, though by no means as powerful and athletic as his brother John, who— but I think I have sufficiently described him already. There is no girl. Next comes Sam, who is somewhat of a nondescript—a staid, self-contained, stubborn sort of boy. The fourth son is a little boy called Charley, a weird-looking child, all eyes, like a young crow, and who never laughs. Mrs. Freeman is as quiet and unassuming as her husband—at least, where his pastoral authority and sense of theological duty are concerned—is not. She is kind, gentle, most hospitable, a truly Christian lady.

Write at length, and fully, weighing and considering all the facts. Was John Freeman drowned, or murdered,

or spirited away and hidden; or did he run away, or
was he swept off by the tide and picked up by a passing
ship? Consider all the possibilities, and write. When we
were at the depôt together I remember you used to guess
out the mystery of a novel from the first few chapters.
This disappearance is curiously like the first chapter of
a novel. Bring your guessing and solving powers to bear
upon it, and oblige yours truly, SAMUEL WATKINS.

CHAPTER IV.

EVERYONE had given up all hope of ever seeing
my brother again, when one person, if a child
of eight may be called a person, strongly and
continually began to assert that he was alive.
How I became possessed of this conviction I
now proceed to relate. It happened in this
manner. On the night of the 31st of July,
exactly three weeks and a day after the disappearance, I had a very singular experience,
which, in spite of all absurd theories of brain-
waves, telepathy, and I know not what, I still
firmly believe to have been an instance of Divine
interposition.

It was upon a Wednesday night, as I particularly remember, because my father always
had service on Wednesday nights, and I had
been to church and returned with the rest of

the family. I went to bed as usual at half-past seven in good health, if not in good spirits. Truly, during those weeks we were all terribly afflicted and cast down. Between eight and nine o'clock, as I lay wide awake, I saw, not a dream, but a clear waking vision!

At the time I was not thinking of Jack at all. I had just got into bed, and was lying on my back and looking upwards into the dark. I became aware of a light not far from me on the left, and thought at first that someone had come into the room with a lamp. Turning a little to one side, I saw a fire burning red and smoky, from which went up a good many sparks. This was all I saw at first, but presently I became aware that someone was sitting near it with his back towards me, bare-headed, and perfectly still.

It was Jack! I sat up and called him by his name, but he made no answer and did not move. Then I asked him a succession of short, quick questions as to what he was doing, why he did not answer me, etc. There was darkness all round the place, darkness which was faintly illuminated by the fire, but afterwards I remembered having seen rough, shiny points of ragged rock on which the firelight faintly played and flickered. I did see clearly a large fish which lay beside him on a flagstone close to the fire. To judge by his attitude he appeared to be gazing intently into the heart of the blaze. Once he stooped forward a little as if to feed the fire.

Still shouting questions I sprang from my bed and rushed towards him, intending to lay my hand on his shoulder. Then I came violently into collision with something solid; it was a wardrobe which stood against the wall on the other side of the room in front of my bed. Recovering myself, I could see the vision still before me as clear and distinct as if I saw it with my eyes; indeed, I have not the least doubt that I did see it with my eyes. Then soft arms were laid round me and I was raised up. It was my mother, who had run upstairs hearing my cries.

She put me back in my bed. The whole family had rushed to the room, greatly frightened by my screamings and loud excited talk. Though there were candles in the room I still saw the apparition, vision, or whatever it might be called, and, still urging my mother and brothers to see it too, was deposited in bed, and even forcibly held down there. When I was again able to look in the same direction the vision was gone!

Of course, my mother concluded at once that I was ill, labouring perhaps under an acute gastric attack, the commencement of a gastric fever, and I was treated on the assumption that I was suffering from that common child's malady, and dosed with the usual medicines. My mother was surprised in the morning to find no sign of illness upon me, and still more so when the doctor declared that I was perfectly well.

Though I was kept in bed my brothers were permitted to see me. Of course I told and told over and over again the whole story of the vision.

"Jack is alive somewhere," I kept saying, "and must be searched for."

"Why do you go on like that, Charley?" they said. "Don't you know he's dead? It was a dream."

"It was no dream," I answered; "I was as broad awake as you are. I saw him, and how could I see him if he wasn't alive?"

"But how could he be in the room? There's no trace of fire here. How can you be so foolish?"

"No," I replied, "he wasn't in the room, of course. When I struck the press which stands against the wall here, I could see him still beyond me. So, of course, he wasn't in the room. But he was somewhere else, and I saw him, and he's alive."

On the following night, shortly after the big mahogany clock in the lobby had struck eight, I continued to watch intently for the reappearance of the vision. Nothing came, however, though I heard the clock strike nine. But on the following night I had an experience quite as surprising to myself, though not to others, as that vision of the fire and of my brother sitting between me and it.

A few minutes after the clock struck, I seemed to grow suddenly and curiously cold, and while still staring out into the darkness, I was aware of the words " The Devil's Parlour " coming into my mind. I did not hear the words at all with my ears. It was as if my mind had ears, and that I heard the words in that way, very clear and distinct, but not at all as if spoken by any audible voice. I did not cry out or make any noise on this occasion, but resolved to stay awake and tell my brothers when they came to bed.

I fell asleep, however, before they came up. In the morning I awoke them and told what had happened. They treated me as little Joseph was treated by his brothers ; nevertheless I saw them look significantly at one another.

After breakfast and before school hours they went off together, Ned taking his cornopean with him. The Devil's Parlour was an awe-inspiring cleft, the opening to some deep and mysterious subterranean hollow, in the side of a long hill which lay about a mile westward from the Rectory. As I afterwards learned, my two brothers went to the cleft, shouted down into it both together, and Ned blew his cornet-à-piston, mouth downwards, awaking huge echoes and reverberations there. Then they listened but heard no reply.

They hardly spoke to me at all after this, and never about my mysterious visions and experiences. The same day I took from the sideboard in the dining-room a great home-made brown cake, and going off by myself rolled it down the Devil's Parlour. Two days afterwards I took and rolled down another, and continued to tell everyone that Jack was alive and in the Devil's Parlour.

I had rolled down some half a dozen cakes in this manner when my mother, who was aware of the rapid disappearance of her cakes, discovered me in the act of making off with one. That night she and my father had a consultation on my case, and the following day I was sent off to an uncle and aunt who lived in an adjoining county. Of course my parents thought that my mind was affected, and my mother attributed it to excessively long school hours and too much brain-work.

At my uncle's, I had nothing to do but amuse myself, and gradually I began to think that perhaps what my uncle and aunt said was true, and that these experiences were only dreams and "lively imaginations," which was the expression used. I was to come home at Christmas, but early in November a messenger arrived with a letter from Ned addressed to my uncle, telling him to send me home at once. Something very strange had occurred in the meantime, something that caused my visions and voice to be regarded at home in quite a new light.

CHAPTER V.

IN the month of October, long after the public
excitement caused by the disappearance of my
brother John had subsided, and even after the
local interest caused by Charley's curious behaviour and conversation had died away, the
suspicion, indeed the conviction, that John had
met with foul play, while it renewed the general
excitement, made our own grief only the deeper
and more bitter. Everyone believed now that
my brother had been murdered.

Du-Corrig, where Jack was last seen, was
not within sight of any house in the neighbourhood, but there was a house and farm close by,
occupied by a returned Irish-American called
Melody, a very big, noisy, and quarrelsome man,
given to drink. He was poor now, though when
he came home he had money. His wife was

dead. He lived here with his mother, who was
bed-ridden, and three children, the eldest of
them called Dannie, who was a pupil in my
father's parochial school.

No one liked Melody; nor am I surprised—
his ways were so different from those of the
rest of the people. One day I overheard a
labourer on the Glebe say to another, " Melody
is drinking again, wherever he got the money."
I noticed the remark, for on the previous evening I had seen him staggering home from the
adjoining village. He endeavoured to get into
conversation with me, but I stepped out, and
could hear him bawling some impertinence after
me. Melody had money and was drinking.
The fact caused a good deal of interest and
curiosity in the neighbourhood.

A few evenings later the schoolmaster called
at the Glebe and inquired for me. I went into
the kitchen and noticed that his face was fixed
and pale; I brought him into the dining-room
and asked him whether he was ill. He said
" No," and was silent. I too was silent and

D

only looked at him. He had a piece of paper
in his hand which he kept twirling between
his fingers in a nervous manner. At last he
said suddenly—

"I came about Master John. I fear, sir,
there has been foul play. You know I taught
him mathematics for his Michaelmas examination last year, and was a good deal with him
in the evenings. He then showed me his ring.
It had a Latin inscription on the inside. Not
knowing Latin, I do not rightly recollect the
words, though I read them at the time and he
translated them for me. Master Edward! Master
Edward!" he cried in great agitation, and laying
the paper on the table, "are those they?"

"They are!" said I. We stood trembling
and looked at each other. Written on the
paper in a large schoolboy hand were the words
"*Nec sperne duritiam.*" Those were the words
engraved on the inside of my brother's ring.

"This is terrible, Mr. Gloster," I said at
last; "tell me all." He did so, and to the
following effect :—

Dannie Melody, it seems, came to school one day looking very big and important, and behaved so badly that he had to be punished. The boy's singular behaviour arose from the fact that he was the possessor of a sixpenny-bit, which he said his father had given to him. As Dannie was never known to have even a halfpenny, his bright sixpence excited a great deal of curiosity, and all the boys were very eager to find out the cause of his father's un-expected munificence. Dannie, however, refused to tell; but, it seems, after having pledged him to fidelity, communicated the secret to a little friend of his.

One day Mr. Gloster surprised these two friends idling at their desk, or, rather, examin-ing together a piece of strange paper. Before Dannie could conceal it Mr. Gloster had snatched it up and demanded of Dannie where he had got the characters with which it was inscribed. They recalled to him the legend in the ring. The boy began to cry, and said that he could not tell, that his father would beat him if he

D 2

did. When school was dismissed Mr. Gloster
kept Dannie back, and at length got the secret
from him.

Dannie, it seems, coming home one day
found his father sitting by the fire and examining a gold ring. The moment the boy
appeared he put it hastily into his pocket. He
came back drunk from the village that night,
and slept long the next morning.

Dannie, with a child's inquisitiveness,
searched his father's pockets till he found the
ring, and after examining it curiously for a long
time, finally the whim seized him of copying
out the strange words which he found on the
inside. He kept the copy and put the ring back
in the pocket from which he had taken it.

When his father awoke and got up, he called
him outside of the house and said to him,
" Dannie, you saw a ring with me last night.
Well, you're to tell no one about it. If you
do, I'll break every bone in your body." Then
he gave Dannie the sixpence as a bribe and
made him give a solemn promise of secrecy.

That was all Dannie had to tell, except that
his father the same day went to our nearest
market town, Ballymohur, and sold the ring
there, as Dannie believed, for he came back
with money, but without the ring.

Mr. Gloster wished to know from me whether
he should tell all this to my parents. Terrible
as was the news, and great as would be the
shock to them, especially to my poor mother,
I thought so. Of the effect upon them I shall
say nothing. Later on in the evening, Mr.
Gloster and I set out for the house of Mr.
Watkins, the sub-inspector of police. When
Mr. Watkins heard this strange story he resolved to arrest at once Melody and his son. A
warrant was procured from the nearest magistrate,
and about nightfall we came to Melody's cabin.

The cabin was absurdly small to be the abode
of such a big man. The thatch was secured by
hay ropes, held in their place by stones attached
to their ends, a row of which hung all round
the cabin under the eaves like a necklace.

The tenant's huge conor rod reposed against

the roof and stretched away into the sky. Everything about the place was as untidy and unkempt as possible. Melody had learned nothing good, but much bad, during his sojourn in the great Republic.

The cabin stood a little distance in from the boreen which led from the high road down the steep valley and ended near Du-Corrig.

As we approached, the big Irish-American issued in a stooping attitude from the little dark doorway, and came along the causeway which crossed the bawn, that is to say the small yard lying in front of the cabin. When he saw us a visible change of expression passed over his face.

One of the constables, showing him the warrant, laid his hand on his shoulder, saying at the same time, " I arrest you in the name of the Queen ! "

" What for ? " said he, looking very angry.

" For the murder of John Freeman," was the reply.

Melody turned pale and staggered. " Gentlemen," he said, " I am not guilty ; I never did it."

"Melody," said the sub-inspector, "Mr. Freeman's ring was seen in your possession. You may make any statement or explanation that you please, but I warn you that what you say will be used against you hereafter at your trial."

"Gentlemen," said Melody, "I'll tell you all I know about that ring. One morning I sees a flock of pigeons in the black field beyant there that has the heap of white stones in the middle of it. I crept under the fence, and when I got near threw a stone or two at them. They fled away, but wan of them flew so bad and sat down again so soon that I followed after and killed her. The ring was fastened to her leg with a bit of cord, and I was afeard that some-one would claim it on me, so I tould Dannie not to tell."

"And the ring, where is it?" said Mr. Watkins sternly.

Melody hesitated for a moment or two; then he said boldly—

"Sir, I losht it."

I perceived at once, and everyone there perceived too, that he lied. The pigeon story, too, though told so circumstantially, we of course disbelieved. Dannie was arrested too, and led away crying bitterly. Melody was lodged in the county gaol, and the boy taken in charge by the police lest his evidence should be in any way tampered with pending the trial.

Melody's cabin was searched by the police, but without discovering there any further evidence of his guilt. It was, however, now recalled that something like a fracas had occurred between my brother and the Irish-American on the evening before the disappearance. That was the evening of my brother's return from Dublin. He arrived unexpectedly by the post-car from Ballymohur and walked home from the village, *i.e.*, Dunbeacon, which was only some three-quarters of a mile from the Rectory.

As he was leaving the village, Melody was seen to join him, he being then in a tipsy condition. What occurred between them in the

way of conversation was not heard, but after a
while my brother was seen to give him a strong
push, not a blow, which sent him staggering
across the road so that he fell into the gripe.
Jack walked on then, taking no further notice
of him. Jack said nothing of this affair to any
of us. I suppose he considered it a trifle.

Of the subsequent investigations and inquiries of the police I shall say little. Their
theory of course was that Melody on the
evening of the disappearance had joined my
brother in the dusk of the evening, had struck
and stunned him there on Du-Corrig, rifled the
body and flung it into the water. Melody's
arrest took place on the 15th of October, and
of course created a great deal of excitement over
the whole country.

A detective came down from Dublin, but no
further evidence was discovered against Melody
save indeed the ring itself. This was found with
a jeweller in Ballymohur, and at once surrendered
to the police. The jeweller, Mr. Campion,
admitted that he had bought it from Melody,

who had previously sold him a watch and other trinkets which he said he had brought home with him from America. I drove into town with Mr. Watkins and at once identified the ring.

The constabulary were still searching for further evidences of Melody's guilt when something happened which in all probability was the means of saving an innocent man's life, namely, complete corroboration of Melody's incredible story about the pigeon and the ring.

CHAPTER VI.

EDWARD FREEMAN'S NARRATIVE (*continued*).—
JACK'S CARRIER PIGEON.

ONE morning in the middle of October, as I
looked from my bedroom window while dressing,
I saw a flock of pigeons, of the slate-coloured
variety common on this coast, fly over the lawn,
and swooping a little, as if they would alight in
an adjoining field, which had been tilled that
summer. I felt a strong desire to have a shot
at them, though I had not once taken out a gun
since Jack's disappearance. Our only gun, by
the way, was Jack's, a long single-barrelled
muzzle-loader. I charged it quickly, passed
through the wood, and surveying the field
from a distance, saw the flock moving about
and feeding in the dark-coloured tillage. I
crept round the fence of the field till I came
within shot of them as I judged. Waiting

till I had three in a line, I fired and killed all three.

As I was bringing them home in triumph, I noticed a piece of linen wrapped round the leg of one of the birds, and fastened by a cord. I cut the cord, and unwinding the linen rag found it was the corner of a handkerchief, and bore certain initials. They were Jack's, viz., J.F. For a moment I stood rooted to the spot, then in a frenzy of joy ran to the house and rushed into the breakfast-room, where the whole family was already assembled at prayers, crying, or I dare say screaming, "Jack is alive."

Again I pass over the agitation of our family circle, for such things are not easy to write about. We now saw that Melody's story of the ring was true. It was evident that Jack, imprisoned somewhere, and without other means of communicating with us, had hit upon this plan. That Jack was alive when he sent out these carriers was plain, but was he alive now? Perhaps the messengers had been despatched by him shortly after his disappearance, and before hunger had made an end of him.

My little brother Charley's vision then was true. My parents bitterly reproached themselves for not having given heed to that strange vision which they now regarded as a special and miraculous interposition of Providence.

I advised that Charley should be sent for at once, in order that we might examine him more carefully about what he had seen. The coachman saddling one of the horses galloped off straight, taking with him a note to my uncle hastily scribbled, and just caught the mail car which was on the point of starting from the village of Dunbeacon. He returned the next day, bringing Charley with him.

Meantime the police and coastguards were communicated with, and the whole country-side was in motion. I and my next brother Sam, attended by some workmen, went off at once to the hill in which was the Devil's Parlour. We had with us a candle and matches and a very long rope. When we arrived there I knotted

the end of the rope round my chest, first
padding it with a blanket lest it should hurt
me, and bade them lower me into the cleft.

Soon I was in dense darkness. The flue, if
I may call it so, was at first crooked and ragged,
then descended sheer, so that I was in mid-air
and could touch nothing with my hands. At
another time I might have been afraid, but the
hope of rescuing Jack drove out fear.

At length I felt my feet touch ground,
gravel as I knew by the feel and the noise. I
shouted, but there was no response. I struck a
match and lit my candle. Almost the first
thing I saw was Charley's cakes lying about. I
did not count them; had I done so the
discovery and rescue of Jack might have come
sooner and by a different way.

The place in which I now found myself was
not what I expected. It was like a great round
room, walled with rock, and paved with stones
and gravel. There were bones of animals here,
and the cakes which poor Charley fancied had
been eaten by Jack. I gave the pre-arranged

"SOON I WAS IN DENSE DARKNESS" (*p.* 46).

signal, viz., a strong jerk at the rope, and was slowly drawn up out of this dark den. Till now we all believed that the Devil's Parlour was a huge subterranean cavern.

Five miles further on towards the west there was a similar cleft leading into another cavern of unknown depth.

We went thither, and I descended that too. Here I went near to being drowned. It communicated with the sea, and was filled at the bottom with salt water. Without seeing it, I was lowered into it, and in fact fell in with a souse. By the slackness of the rope those above concluded that I had reached the bottom. Though I tugged vigorously at the rope they were not aware of it. I could not tug strongly while I was swimming, and then the great length of rope rendered it, I suppose, less sensitive. Here, too, all the way down and up again I shouted at intervals and heard no response. It was night when we returned home.

No sign of Jack had been discovered by any-one that day. The coastguards had been out

since morning visiting the rocks and islands, of
which there were several in the neighbourhood,
but had been as unsuccessful as myself.

When I awoke next day, it seemed to me
that I had caught a very bad cold. I got up
nevertheless, but the moment my mother saw me
she ordered me to my room. I refused to go,
and my father had to exert his parental authority
in a very stern manner before I could be got to
obey. In the afternoon Charley arrived. I was
aware of the fact, but of little more, for by this
time the fever had so grown upon me that I was
beginning to be unconscious.

After this I remember no more till I began
to be convalescent after an attack of brain-fever.
The searching for Jack had gone on without me
during the remainder of October and the beginning of November while I lay at death's door.
But the searchers had found no sign or trace of
my brother. The police were utterly nonplussed.
I heard that a very clever detective had been
sent down from Dublin, but after wasting a fortnight had returned, saying that we were all mad.

I heard, too, that during all these weeks little Charley regularly every second day, wet or fine, used to go to the Devil's Parlour, and roll down his brown cake. My mother made no objection.

He still continued to do it even after I began to move about, and after I had declared to him that there was nothing at the bottom of the cavern but gravel, bones, and the bread which he was wasting. I began to think of forcibly restraining him from this practice, for it was killing my mother, who used to weep for a long time after she had given him his cake and seen him off. The neighbours watched him with the utmost compassion, and indeed I have never seen anything so pathetic.

"Was it said in your dream that Jack was in the Devil's Parlour?" I asked him.

"No," he said, "but I believe that he is there without being told; I told myself."

When I was sufficiently convalescent to be able to move about again, I organised a search-party of my own. I believe we visited every

E

cave and nook along the coast for fifteen miles
on either side of Du-Corrig.   We searched also
the islands and isolated rocks out in the sea,
though they had been already searched by the
coastguards.

CHAPTER VII.

EDWARD FREEMAN'S NARRATIVE (*continued*).—

MYSTERIOUS DISAPPEARANCE OF EDWARD FREEMAN.

THAT Jack was or had been in some cavern I knew. These slate-coloured pigeons—blue rocks, as they are called—roost in caves. Indeed, we never called them anything but cave-pigeons. But where was the cave? It now occurred to me that Jack, having hooked some unusually large fish (the sun-fish, for example, could do it), had been drawn into and under the sea. I knew that under such circumstances he would not let go his rod, and thought it possible that while under the water he had been sucked through a submarine tunnel into some unknown and otherwise unapproachable interior cavern, and had been unable to re-discover or retrace the passage by which he had entered.

E 2

This cavern, I thought, might communicate with the open air, or with one of the many ordinary caves or fissures along the coast by some narrow outlet, through which his carrier pigeons might have escaped. Improbable as was this theory, it was the most probable that I could frame, and was, in fact, rather near truth. All the theories and surmises of the police contained one or more incredible assumptions.

I procured the services of the same diver who had been formerly employed by Mr. Watkins. For more than three weeks under my superintendence he made submarine searchings, of the kind indicated, on either side of Du-Corrig, and to a considerable distance each way. All was, however, in vain. The diver gave up first. He said it was a sin to waste any more of my father's money in such an attempt. With my father's sanction I now wrote to the Board of Works in Dublin, asking them to send me another. Harris, the man whom I employed, obstinately refused to go on with the search. This diver

was actually on his way down from Dublin,
when——"

[When, in fact, Edward Freeman himself disappeared just as suddenly and unaccountably as
his brother.—EDITOR.]

CHAPTER VIII.

You will no doubt have already read the official report in which I have informed the authorities of the disappearance of the Rev. Mr. Freeman's second son under circumstances somewhat similar to those which attended the disappearance of the eldest, Mr. John Freeman. This extraordinary event has caused a degree of consternation and alarm over the whole countryside which it would be impossible to describe.

On the morning of Friday last, about ten o'clock, Edward Freeman—whose exertions for the discovery of his brother's place of conceal-ment, voluntary or enforced, have been so inde-fatigable—was seen walking in the direction of Du-Corrig, and no doubt on his way to that fatal and ill-omened rock. Two children coming along the main road saw him turn aside and step briskly down the little lane or boreen leading to

Du-Corrig   He had a fishing-rod on his shoulder and a box of bait in his hand.   He has not been seen since.

The mystery is infinitely more than doubled by this second disappearance, for with it our hypothesis regarding the first, viz., that Melody murdered John Freeman, vanishes too.   I declare I begin to think there is something supernatural and uncanny in the whole of this Freeman affair. All other theories having failed, I can assure you, though I may earn nothing but your contempt by the avowal, that I find my thoughts straying perpetually in the direction of supernaturalism as that which may supply us with the key to this astounding mystery.

A singular superstition of old standing, but which was believed to have died out, has been revived amongst the people to account for this disappearance of the brothers.   It is said that the coast is haunted by what the English-speaking fishermen call a *worm*, and the Irish-speaking a *piast*.   Even before the disappearance of Edward Freeman, I overheard talk of this *piast* in

connection with John Freeman's disappearance,
but when I laughingly desired more definite information on the subject I was refused.

As you are aware, when I was first stationed
in this district I determined, for professional
reasons, to learn the language in which the
people express their most intimate thoughts, that
is to say, the old Gaelic tongue. It has been very
useful to me. I have always found that the
people are much more communicative and con-
fiding with a person who can speak to them in
this ancient language. Concerning the *piast*,
however, on this occasion referred to I found the
men, whom I had overheard speaking, sullenly
and obstinately uncommunicative. I am certain,
however, that the notion of a supernatural and
man-devouring monster now haunting these
shores is universal amongst the island and coast
population.

Since John Freeman was lost, not a man has
been seen fishing upon any of the rocks along
the coast, and since Edward disappeared in the
same equally amazing manner, no fishing boat

from our little basin has ever remained out after dark. For myself I must say that, although of course I do not believe in any such nonsense, yet for some days I have found my imagination most disagreeably haunted by the thought of this reptile prowling round the shore and seeking whom he may devour. I have dreamed of the brute, and that he had plucked me too—not from off a rock, but out of my flower-garden, as I was watering my flowers.

The beast seemed to be a monstrous serpent with wings and a hairy mane. He raised himself out of the sea, and, looking all around with his basilisk eyes, suddenly swooped down upon me and seized me. I screamed so loud that the whole household came running to my room. You can imagine what a fool I seemed to myself and others. On Friday, in the forenoon, I say, the second young Freeman was lost.

Of what we have done and attempted in the meantime you will find enough in the official report. The following is for your private eye, for I know you take an interest in these queer

superstitions which still linger amongst the
peasantry and fisher people, and which are, I
suppose, a remnant of paganism.

On Sunday afternoon I saw a four-oared boat
endeavouring to gain the long island where you
and I made such a bag of rabbits last summer,
and which the people call Lan-wohr. Curious
to see whether the rowers could accomplish
their purpose against the head-wind which blew
strongly from the west, I kept watching them.
The boat had started early that morning from
the little fishing village of Coos-beg, which lies
to the east of our own village, Dunbeacon, and
some ten miles distant from my place.

Suddenly the boat's head was turned towards
land, a sail hoisted, and the boat came driving
straight towards my own private little harbour,
Coos-an-Dorcha, which of course you remember.

The boat seemed to me as if fleeing from
the pursuit of an enemy, so furiously she came
plunging along with the water leaping and
boiling at her bows. I went down to the strand
to meet the crew. When they were landed

and had drawn up their boat, I bade the men step up to my house and have refreshment before going to the village. They intended to sleep there that night and go on next morning to Lan-wohr should the wind come down or change its direction.

They were in all six Lan-wohr men, very wild and rough in appearance, but, like all the remote islanders along this coast, by no means so wild as they looked. Indeed, these islanders are almost invariably a simple-minded, peaceable, hospitable, and kindly people.

I gave them a comforting draught of undiluted whisky as they sat and dried themselves around a big fire in my kitchen, and afterwards regaled them with plenty of home-made cake and butter and big bowls of steaming hot tea. They were much exhausted from rowing, and the poor fellows looked so happy and pleased as they ate and drank, that it was a delight only to see the look of satisfaction in their simple countenances. Then at my suggestion they took out their pipes and smoked, I, too, smoking with them and asking many questions in Gaelic.

They were at first very friendly and communicative; then I spoke of the disappearance of Mr. Freeman's sons, of the fruitlessness of all our searchings, and observed, with as serious and awe-struck a face and manner as I could assume, that they might have been snatched from Du-Corrig by a *worm*.

A sudden silence thereupon fell on the Lanwohr men. One of them made some answer which I forget, but the subject was not pursued. I felt at once that the Lan-wohr men knew a great deal more about the *piast* than they thought good to communicate to me, who, though I could speak their tongue, was yet a gentleman, a Sassenagh, and, in short, not one of themselves. As you are aware, these people consider it "unlucky" to talk more than is necessary about the supernatural things and personages in whom they believe, and will never speak about them with those who are not quite in accord and sympathy with themselves upon such subjects. The peasantry who are communicative on such subjects will be found, almost invariably, to be persons who have to some extent become emancipated from these forms of superstition.

When the men rose to leave for the village, which they offered to do, not too soon and also not too long after they had partaken of my hospitality, I bade the oldest of them, a gigantic old fisherman called Crohoor-beg, to stay with me for the night, for I could spare him a bed. He consented, and remained when the rest took their leave.

He was called Crohoor-beg, or Crohoor the Little, no doubt ironically on account of his great size. I had noticed that when I alluded to the *piast* Crohoor's face became unusually rigid and impassive, and that he closed his mouth as if resolved not to speak again that evening. I now led Crohoor into my office, stirred up the fire, made a good blaze, and after some allusion to the hardship which he had endured that day, brewed for him a stiff tumbler of punch.

Though he was now in my own private room, and surrounded by pictures and many strange things savouring of "quality life," Crohoor's behaviour was almost gentlemanlike; at least, it was characterised by ease, simplicity, and dignity. Later on I spoke again of the disappearance of Mr. Freeman's sons, of the great affliction of the family, and of the exertions of myself and my man to solve the mystery. Eventually Crohoor-beg broke through his reserve, and before he lay down that night told me all he knew or believed about the *piast.*

CHAPTER IX.

MR. WATKINS' NARRATIVE (*continued*).—THE PIAST.

CROHOOR-BEG commenced by informing me,
somewhat in the manner of a professional story-
teller or historian about to deliver a lecture, that
Ireland was at one time filled with monstrous
reptiles, ugly and horrible, which preyed upon
the people. So much I knew, and also that St.
Patrick had banished them, all but a few which
lingered on after his time in remote mountain
lakes; but Crohoor said that though this might
be true of other parts of the country, it was not
St. Patrick who had banished the great *piast* of
this region, but a man called Cuhoolin. The
name of the *piast*, he said, was Cooree, and that
after a terrible battle Cuhoolin had conquered
her, driven her into the sea, and put her under
spells to remain there till the Day of Judgment,
when, according to Crohoor, she will be cast for
ever into Hell, and the door shut. Also

Cuhoolin put spells upon her that she should not have power to eat men, only once and again and between times.

Crohoor went on to inform me that when his father was a little boy some men had been lost while fishing off this coast, and it was believed they had been eaten by the *piast*. A panic took possession of the whole country, so that fishing ceased. There was at the time in this country a very good and holy priest, who had unusual influence over the minds of the people. He held a sea-service and celebrated mass upon the water, in the midst of a great flotilla of boats, for the banishment of the monster. After that he forbade the people even to speak of the *piast*, not even to mention her as a thing of the past, an old-time plague upon the coast; and such was his influence, according to Crohoor, that, for two generations, only the vaguest ideas circulated amongst the people concerning the reptile. Since the taking away of Mr. John Freeman from Du-Corrig, "the old people had been talking"; "and why shouldn't they," he added,

" when 'tis plain that the *piast* is alive and strong and at her old bloody work again ? "

" What is the appearance of the *piast ?* " I asked ; " and where does she live ? "

" I'll tell you about that, sir," he said ; and proceeded to relate the following story, with regard to which I may add that I am very conscious that my English does not adequately express the power and picturesqueness of Crohoor's Gaelic.

" These things happened before my father's time and before my grandfather's, but they are as true as that you are sitting in that chair. Two men and a gossoon went in a boat from Lan-beg, which lies a little westward from Lanwohr (but your honour knows the island), to buy flour in Dunbeacon, for little is the grain grown there on Lan-beg by reason of the stony floor of the island. The wind was from the south'ard, so they hoisted sail, and it wasn't long before they made the Basin and grounded their boat there. When they bought the flour and put the bags in the boat, it was the

F

judgment of one of the men that they should run down the boat, hoist sail, and return to Lan-beg immediately, so that the daylight might be with them in their returning.

" ' None of your nonsense,' says the other. ' It isn't once in six months I come to the city, and I won't leave it till I warm myself well with water of life.'

" ' Water of death,' says the other. ' 'Tis unlucky to be passing the square hole after dark at any time, and in especial on this night.'

" The night, your honour, was All Hallows' Eve, and 'tis a night when all the infernal things in the world, from the Devil down, have great power, be the reason what it may.

" ' The *piast* be hanged,' says the other. ' I hold by no such foolishness.'

" The man who said this word was called Teigue Rue. He had red hair, and was the biggest and strongest man on the little island, and a terror to the peaceably inclined. By the same token, too, he had gone away to be a sailor

when he was a slip, and he went to many out-
landish parts before he came home and settled
himself down with his kin, for good and all, in
Lan-beg. And though he used to pretend to
laugh at the old stories of the people, he himself
had a custom of talking of some sea-devil or *piast*
that he called Ould Davy, and sometimes Davy
with another name that the old people did not
remember.

"And so now all that his comrade could say
was no use, but back he would go to the public-
house, taking his comrade with him, who was a
weak man, and there they were diverting
themselves till the going-down of the sun.
The comrade's name was Shaun. He was an
O'Flaherty by nation. Well, Teigue Rue,
though he laughed at the notion of the *piast*, had
too much sense to get drunk and he about to go
out on the salt water in a sail-boat, or to allow
Shaun O'Flaherty to get drunk either, though
the people said afterwards that Shaun, in spite
of his desire for an early return, was then all for
more drink and another song.

" They pushed the boat down after that, and stepped the mast and hoisted the sail, with the night upon them, and the moon rising three-quarter over the Ballyhourahan hills there in the east. Teigue Rue took the bailing-can and dipped it in the tide and poured the salt water on his head to cool himself after the liquor, and make his intellect more steady and considerate, and he made Shaun do the same. The gossoon also was warm and pleasant in himself, for he was with them in the public-house and all through. The stars came out, but though the night was bright and fine the wind blew strong still from the south'ard.

" Well, sir, the boat was just opposite your own coos, called Coos-an-Dorcha by reason of the high black rocks around it and the shadow that is there always, when the wind scanted of a sudden, in an unreasonable manner, and the sail began to flap.

" ' It would be better to go back,' says Shaun.

" ' It would be better to do no such thing,'

says Teigue Rue. 'Handle your oar, man, and let the gossoon take the helm, and we won't be long in making Lan-beg, for the sea is like a goose-pond. The tide is against us here, but it won't be against us a mile farther on, and we can get home from that without inconvenience.'

"Well, they rowed on in that manner till they came opposite the square hole in the big straight cliff."

"What hole is that?" said I.

"I'm surprised your honour has not noticed it," replied Crohoor; "but, indeed, unless it was pointed out to him a person might not see it."

"I never saw or heard of it," I said.

"Your honour knows the big straight cliff between your coos and Du-Corrig?"

"Certainly," I said; "but I am a little short-sighted, and never noticed that hole."

"Well, sir, up high in that cliff there is a square hole, and big enough too, though it looks small from the water. They were nearing this place when Shaun O'Flaherty stopped rowing and crossed himself and said—

"'Teigue Rue, I'm greatly afraid.'

"'Afraid of what?' says Teigue Rue.

"'Of the *piasta-wohr*,' he says; 'sure, this is her favourite locality, between Du-Corrig and the Coos-an-Dorcha (that is to say, the Black Rock and the Coos of Darkness), and sure, they say that it is through Cooree's Window she comes out, and goes in again through the same, and has her nest there.'

"Then Teigue Rue spoke words about the *piast*, and, though I well remember them, I won't say them in your honour's presence; and he fell to beating Shaun O'Flaherty to make him quit his nonsense and be rowing the same as formerly. Then the gossoon screamed, with an awful and terrible cry that was heard by all the people of the valley that runs up back from Du-Corrig, and the men stopped their fighting and looked where the boy was looking, and that was up at the big white cliff.

"Then they saw something that was enough

to kill them all at once with the fright. From
Coorce's Window the *piast* was coming out.
And first she raised her head up along the cliff-
side, stretching herself like a serpent or a huge
black eel, and the head continued going up till
it passed beyond the cliff-top, so that they could
see the head of the *piast* against the sky and the
stars, and her body all the time working slowly
out of the hole. She was maned like a horse
and had ears like a horse, and her eyes were like
two red fires in her head.

"In that manner she raised her head up
among the stars, and then, making an arch with
her neck, turned her eyes downward, and at first
she did not see them, but stretched her head
along the cliff shore to Du-Corrig, and then
backwards along the coast as far as Coos-an-
Dorcha, and into the coos, winding her head and
neck round the rock at the mouth of the coos.
After that she raises her head again, but not so
high as before, and in the bright water she sees the
black boat, and without hurry, comes down upon
it, the two men sitting there without a word, as

silent and as steady as stones, with faces like
white paper. Then with her long tongue she
reaps them into her mouth—they still without
a word or noise—and chews them very deliber-
ately.

"The cracking of their bones in the mouth
of the *piast*, that boy used to say afterwards,
was like the crackling of 'brusna' in a fire, and
that the shower of blood that fell from her jaws
along the hairs of her mouth—every hair as
long as an oar—was like the sound of hail upon
water. And after that she raised up her head to
swallow them more conveniently, after the
manner of birds when they drink."

"Then the boy escaped?" I said.

"Yes, sir, the boy escaped. When the *piast*
raised her head to swallow the two men, God
gave him courage so that he slipped over the
gunwale of the boat upon the seaward side, and
sheltered himself so. It was not long before
the *piast* came down again. The boy did not
see her on account of the place where he was,
but he heard her breathing and smelt the breath

of her, like sea-weed, only very strong, and it is astonishing how he contrived to keep himself afloat considering the great fear that was upon him. She returned to the boat twice after that, for no doubt she smelt him, and he knew her coming on each occasion by reason of the breathing and of the very strong smell. In the end he heard a loud noise, and he said to himself that it was the noise of the hinder parts of the *piast* falling into the water, and that he would be safer in the boat now than in the sea. Accordingly, though with very great difficulty, owing to the fear that was upon him, he climbed over the gunwale and gathered the sail around him and lay down in the bottom of the boat.

"The boat was picked up next morning by the Coos-beg men, for she was carried eastward by the tide, and when they unrolled the sail the boy was an idiot, and he continued in that state, and languishing besides, till the eve of St. John's Day in the next year, when he died, saving only that for nine days before his death

his understanding returned to him, and he told
the story many times to different people."

"Is it your opinion then," I said, "that the
piast has taken the two young gentlemen, my
neighbours?"

"God alone," said Crohoor, "knows that,
with Whom is the knowledge of all things. But
if it be so, and the *piast* has them, Heaven be
our defence, for the power of man and the mind
of man furnish no protection against the like of
her."

"Crohoor, you said a short time ago that a
man beat that reptile in battle, and banished her
into the rocks and the sea?"

"So I said, sir, but it is thought that the
man who did it was more than a man, and that
though he lived before the coming of St. Patrick,
yet the power of the Almighty was in him."

Such, my friend, is the explanation of the
disappearance of the two brothers offered by
Crohoor-beg, O'Brien "by nation," who stands
six feet three and a half in his stockings, and
is of a size and bulk corresponding, a poor

fisherman and cottier of the island called Lan-
wohr, who can't speak English and never read a
line in any printed book, but who, I verily believe, is not only a nobler and better, but a wiser
man, too, than most of the professional men with
whom I am acquainted. And though his theory,
being grounded on an incredible superstition, is
to be rejected, it is not at all more irrational than
several which I have heard soberly advanced by
educated persons.—SAMUEL WATKINS.

CHAPTER X.

MR. WATKINS' NARRATIVE (*continued*).—MR.
WATKINS RECEIVES A LETTER FROM THE BROTHERS

MY DEAR HENRY,—This astounding and mysterious tragedy of the disappearance of the brothers Freeman has entered on a phase literally calculated to strike one dumb. In short, we have had a letter from the brothers, and yet we cannot find them. What I now proceed to relate is incredible, yet it is true. After the disappearance of Edward, and after all our renewed searchings and explorations had come to nothing, I argued with myself in the following manner :—Wherever the brothers are, they are doubtless together, and have been spirited away and concealed by the same person and in the same way. From his place of concealment John Freeman was able to send out messenger pigeons with tokens attached. These tokens, though they proved that he was alive, gave us no inkling as to his place of concealment or abode. He may have sent out others to which are attached definite written information. He could have written, in blood, characters on a strip torn from his handkerchief, and by some device protected the characters from the weather. Now that the two brothers are together, the chances are that they have sent out some pigeon so equipped.

At once I wrote off to my two nephews, Harry and Joseph Battersby, whom you must have met last summer, to come without delay to me, bringing their guns with them. I had now determined to shoot every cave-pigeon in this neighbourhood, and I knew that my nephews, being boys, and accustomed to stealing upon and shooting from behind hedges at curlews, starlings, cave-pigeons, and such like, would do far more execution than I could. Having posted the letter, I went forth instanter, and also distributed small shot to my four men at this barrack, bidding them be off and shoot as many cave-pigeons as they could that day. I

recalled their privileges the same evening, for
they only succeeded in frightening the birds and
making them very shy. They did not bring
home a single pigeon, though they were firing
about the country all day. I myself, though I
kept stealing and dodging behind fences and
furze-brakes from ten o'clock to dusk, only shot
two. They bore no token of any kind. I knew
that with the arrival of Harry and Joseph there
would be a different tale to tell. So there
was.

Every day for a week they brought in from
five to twelve pigeons, till a pigeon began to be
a *rara avis* in our country, for those that were
not killed were frightened away. The boys
knew my purpose.

One day, about nine days after their arrival,
Harry came rushing into my office, shouting and
exclaiming and holding a pigeon in his hand,
round whose leg something was tightly wrapped.
I saw that it was linen laced with cord very
tightly along the shank between the bird's claw
and its knee. My hands so trembled with

excitement that I cut myself, and badly, before I cut that cord.

When I unwound the linen and laid it out upon the table I found upon it various stains of red. The linen had certainly been written upon originally, but the rain had penetrated, and melting the red ink—blood no doubt—converted the characters into mere blotches and stains.

I remained alone a long time studying the red daubs and splashes—you can imagine in what a state of mind. This rag of linen held the secret which I verily believe I would have given all my worldly goods to master. I turned it this way and that, for there was nothing to indicate which side should be held uppermost. Then, at last, it seemed to me that in one place I saw a W, after which a mere blotch of red colour representing, apparently, the rest of a word, and at the end of it another W. I called my wife to my assistance. She was sure of the first W but not of the second. Curiously enough, both the boys were sure of the second but not of the

first. I was sure of both myself. As you know,
I am always sure of everything that jumps with
my expectations and hopes. You are a phleg-
matic fellow yourself, Harry, a man of sheer
intellect; but I think that even you, if you had
been through these Freeman experiences, lasting
now for more than five months, with the eyes of
the whole country upon you, might have been,
perhaps, as much excited as I was this evening.
I ran to the shelf for my Webster's dictionary.
Do you remember how when we were sitting
here together last summer after dinner, smoking
and thinking of nothing, a little girl appeared at
the door and said—

"Mrs. Horan's compliments, sir, and would
you lend her the loan of your dictionary, for
she's writing a letter," and how you replied—

"Mr. Watkins' compliments to Mrs. Horan,
and tell her that he has not read it himself
yet"?

Well, it was the same dictionary, and a great
deal of trouble I had to get it out of Mrs.
Horan's clutches.

I turned to the letter W and ran my eye down all the words beginning with that letter in quest of those which ended with the same. *Willow* would suit, so would *window*. There were others, such as *wallow*, etc., but I neglected them. I rang for my orderly and bade him make inquiries amongst the people and learn whether there was any place in this neighbourhood called by a name in which *willow* or *window* occurred.

Now, I had not the least reason for supposing that, even if my assumption was correct, the word which began and ended with W was the name of a place. It might be a verb, it might be anything; but nevertheless, I at once jumped to the conclusion that it was the name of the place where I was to find the brothers.

I had hardly uttered my directions when both my nephews cried out at once—

"Why, Uncle Sam, there's Curry's Window." And Harry, who takes more liberties with me than the other, gave me to understand that we

G

were all "duffers" not to have searched Curry's Window before.

As I had not the least notion of what Curry's Window was, they proceed to enlighten me. Curry's Window, they said, was a little black square hole high up in the face of the smooth sheer cliff which extended from Du-Corrig to my coos.

In short, Curry's Window was the hole out of which the *piast* in Crohoor-beg's story had appeared when she had devoured the two fishermen. This was a curious coincidence, and indeed, as Harry suggested, it was a singular thing that we should have explored the caves in distant islands, yet not have explored this hole which was near Du-Corrig. But then, how could the boys have got thither?—for there is no climbing on that cliff, which starts sheer out of the sea, and is accessible neither by land nor sea.

I brooded over this all night, and the more I thought about it the more absurd did it seem that the brothers should be immured there. It

was just possible, of course, that the brothers
having fallen into the sea, might have been
sucked under by a current and whirled into some
cavern of which Curry's Window was another
aperture. The theory was just imaginable, but
no more. However, as we had tried to work
out so many absurd theories, I thought I might
as well work out this absurd theory too as do
nothing.

Accordingly I laid my plans that night, and
next day had one of my men lowered from the
top of the cliff by a rope. In order to signal
to those who held the rope I went out in
a boat, rowed by the coastguards, who have been
extremely helpful to me in all this business.
Lieutenant Crumps indeed, that steadiest of
church-goers, who never once to my knowledge
missed even the Wednesday evening service, has
taken the matter very coolly. Whenever I refer
to the disappearance of the boys or of the
affliction of the Freeman family, he says in a
formal manner, as if he were answering the
responses, " It is indeed a thousand pities." I

G 2

blazed out on him on the last occasion, which had the effect of waking him up a little. However, I need not complain, for though not actively helpful, he lets me direct the movements of his people, who are extremely sympathetic and active in the matter.

From the water then I signalled to the men, who on the edge of the cliff lowered the explorer to Curry's Window, motioning them to the right or to the left so as to drop their man exactly to the correct point. He was the most active and intelligent of the sub-constables, and went down provided with the means of striking a light and exploring the cavity. We saw him stand in the aperture and signal to us that he should be again lowered.

This we did, and he descended into the interior, where he remained for more than an hour. However, to make a long story short, my sub-constable reported to me in the evening that Curry's Window was the small opening of an enormous underground hollow, with three huge galleries branching off from a vast central space,

and that he had traversed the whole of it, shouting as he went and brandishing his torch. His
description of the vast cavern was so interesting
that my nephews were very anxious to make the
descent themselves, and I promised that next
summer, when you are with me, we should make
up a party and go down with torches, but said
that I was in no mood at present for agreeable
explorations.

I am now again alone in my office writing
this while all the world is wrapped in slumber.
Here nightly I sit cogitating and reflecting like
some stupid old owl on his barn-perch, thinking
and thinking till my mind becomes a perfect
blank. I would consider myself a sheer fool but
for the fact that we had a very sharp Dublin
detective down here for a fortnight, who, after
having sent us on several wild-goose chases,
went away at last declaring that we were all
mad.

What report he sent in to the office I don't
know, but he and my men had words before
parting, and they gave him plainly to understand

that they regarded him as no better than a pre-
tentious ass or " bosthoon."   I fancy that his
report is that John Freeman certainly " ran
away "; and that, let me observe, is what no one
who lives here believes.

CHAPTER XI.

MR. WATKINS' NARRATIVE *(continued)*.—HE
RECEIVES A SECOND AND BETTER LETTER.

I WAS much cast down by these events—my
hopes had been raised so high. At one moment
we seemed to be on the verge of the solution of
this mystery, and now we were as far away from
it as ever. The last pigeon shot, I may observe,
was the sixty-fourth. For some days the boys
had shot none. The pigeons were virtually extir-
minated or banished, and I had deprived the
brothers Freeman of what was apparently their
sole · means of communicating with the world
out of their mysterious prison—and that was
not a pleasant reflection. One evening I and
my nephews (they had just come in empty-
handed, as usual of late) sat here in my office
dumb and stupid for a long time. At last
Harry said—

"It's no use, uncle, going after these pigeons for a good while now. We must give them time to come back. Lend us your rifle : I'd like to have a shot at a seal. There are three or four of them always moving about between your cove and Du-Corrig. I used to see an odd one there last summer, but there seems to be quite a colony of them there now."

"All right, lads," I said; "take the rifle. You will find the boat in the cove. She's small, remember, and easily capsized, so take care of yourselves."

I was anxious to be by myself. The high spirits of the boys, who naturally could not be expected to feel about these matters as I did, were beginning to oppress me. The fact was that my mind—now for so many months absorbed by, and concentrated upon, this extra-ordinary and increasing and expanding mystery —was beginning to be somewhat unhinged. I thought of the lost lads all day, and dreamed of them, perhaps, all night; for certainly I never awoke without being conscious that I had been dreaming about them. I am haunted, too, by poor Mrs. Freeman's wan, sorrow-stricken face. Mr. Freeman, when last I saw him, was bowed in the shoulders—he who used to be as straight as a drilled soldier—and his look was that of an aged man. I, as head of the police in this district, have, of course, been blamed for not doing more; though I confess no word of censure has reached my ears.

But, to resume, I now come to something that will startle and amaze even your philosophic soul.

The boys returned that evening in the dusk. They had seen several seals, and had got a shot at one without doing any execution. I was rather surprised at the number of seals seen by the boys, for, though seals were not uncommon on this coast, such a number as my nephews had seen in the same place was something quite unusual. As we sat at the tea-table, while the boys were talking in an animated manner about the events of the afternoon, and while I could hardly for a single instant keep my thoughts

off the lost brothers, I heard Harry say to my
wife—

"And there was one seal, Aunt Mary, and
every time he came up there was a ball bobbing
in the water behind him, and when he went
down it disappeared."

Instantaneously the thought sprang into my
mind, "Could it be that John Freeman, or John
and Edward, were signalling to us by means of
that seal?"

The supposition was, of course, absurd and
far-fetched. How could they catch a seal, in
the first instance? Nevertheless, the appearance of a seal swimming about with something attached to it was in itself startling
enough.

"I will go out with you in the morning," I
said. "That seal we must shoot."

Early next day, though the wind had risen
and the sea was rough, my nephews and I took
boat together at the Shady Coos and rowed out.
Between the coos and Du-Corrig we saw some
half-dozen seals. Several times I had a good

opportunity of shooting one of them, but did
not shoot. The seal I wanted was not visible.
We came home for early dinner and went out
again immediately after. The boys, who now
knew what I wanted, and who were not short-
sighted like myself, kept a sharp look-out for
the seal of which I was in quest. As we moved
slowly along, Joseph said—

"There is a seal lying on the Corrig-a-
skame rock; that may be *it*, for I remember it
was a small one. Do you see anything behind
him, Harry?"

"No," said Harry, "but it is hard to see
anything in the place where he is lying. When
he begins to move we can see the ball better,
for it will hop and jump somewhere behind
him."

"Row on very slowly, lads," said I.

We were coming from the east, and the seal
was lying on the rock with its head to the west.
The wind, too, was blowing from that direction.

Corrig-a-skame was a long black rock covered

literally all over with little mussels growing as thick as grass. It was invisible at high water, but at low tide stood out pretty well, and resembled the back of a small whale. The name means " The Rock of the Leap." Some active wight in old times had sprung from the corrig to the cliff, or from the cliff to the corrig. It is a common name for such rocks on the west coast. Almost every league of the coast exhibits somewhere a Corrig-a-skame, or a rock called after somebody's leap—Lem-Con, or Lem-Cathal, *i.e.*, Con's Leap, Cathal's Leap, etc.

I bade the boys wrap their handkerchiefs round the leather of the oars to deaden the sound of the rowing, and went to the bow with my rifle. The boys sitting sternward of their oars so as to keep their eyes on the seal, rowed gently forward.

" I am sure it's the same," whispered Harry, who was just behind me ; " and I think I see the ball too. Yes, it is ! " he added, " and I see the ball. Fire at him now, uncle ! "

While I was trying to get a steady aim, which was difficult owing to the rocking of the boat, the creature suddenly turned its head, saw us, and commenced bounding and flapping forwards along the length of the rock, while behind it, as it moved swiftly along, a round ball jumped too. I fired and missed. The creature sent forth a loud mewing sort of cry and splashed into the water on the further side.

" It has left the ball behind ! " cried the two boys together in great excitement.

The truth was that the ball had been caught in some cleft so that the string which connected it with the animal had been broken. None of us saw exactly how it happened, but the creature was gone and the ball remained behind. I could not see it now myself, as it was no longer in motion, but the boys did. We rowed up to the rock, but the surf all around it was so great that we could not land. The wind was steadily rising and the sea beginning to run unpleasantly high. My boat, too, was small and light, not intended to stand rough weather. The tide, however, was flowing, and in a short time I knew that some wave would sweep the ball off the rock.

We kept the boat's head to the wind for about three-quarters of an hour, and at last had the pleasure of seeing one large wave carry the ball clear back off the rock, and a little later the ball had disengaged itself from the surf. You can imagine with what delight I took this waif into my hands. Though there was little rational ground for such a belief, I felt an assurance amounting to conviction that I had in my hands the explanation of the mysterious tragedy. The ball was a small bladder—apparently a sheep's bladder—and was very tightly fastened at the mouth with whip-cord, or strong fishing-line. When the boys looked to see me open it I did nothing of the kind. I bade the boys row, went myself to the tiller, and turned the boat's head home.

I had stayed in the vicinity of Corrig-a-skame too long, and I knew it. I knew that good steering and good luck too were now

required in order to enable us to make my coos.
I did not open the bladder, partly because I did
not desire to remain in this jeopardy a moment
longer than was necessary; and partly because I
wished in the event of an accident befalling us,
that the unopened bladder and its contents
should still be left swimming. The situation,
indeed, was momentarily becoming more serious.
The wind increased to a gale, and the huge
waves lifted the little boat and propelled her
forward like a chip. I feared to bring her
broadside to the wind and waves, yet that was
necessary in order to get into the Shady Coos.
So I steered past it and let her drive forward to
the Basin, a mile further on, the entrance to
which was wide, and did not offer such a sharp
angle to be turned as did my own little
cove.

However, not to be tedious, when I have so
many infinitely more important things to relate,
we made the Basin in safety and drew up our
boat on the coastguard's slip. Bidding the boys
say nothing to anyone about our waif, we three

started for home.　The bladder was in my top-
coat pocket, and I kept my hand upon it during
the walk.　I was in a fever of excitement and
expectation.

When I got home I went straight into my
office by myself, locked the door, cut open the
cord which bound the mouth of the bladder,
ripped the skin up carefully, or as carefully as I
could, with my penknife, and from the interior
took out half a sheet of note-paper.　On one
side was writing in ink.　It was the conclusion
of a letter of no importance; indeed, it was a
tradesman's letter, and signed " John Costello,"
a musical-instrument merchant in our county
town.　On the other side were characters in red,
written with some blunt instrument, like the
pointed end of a match or bit of timber, and at
foot of the writing in larger letters were two
names :—

> JOHN FREEMAN.
> EDWARD FREEMAN.

each name in different hand-writing and representing the signatures of the lads, which I knew.

The body of the red writing was Edward Freeman's. It was to the following effect :—

> "We are here at the bottom of the Devil's Parlour.
> There is a way right down to us. Most of Charley's
> loaves have come down. We came in by the square
> hole high up in the sea-cliff. Both well.
>
> JOHN FREEMAN.
> EDWARD FREEMAN."

By the "square hole!"—the *piast's* hole!—
who could have thought it? The little black
spot far away up in the face of the cliff. And
yet it was through this aperture when he had
been lowered by ropes from the cliff's top that I
despatched my sub-constable, Mulvaney. Mulvaney had then explored with torchlights and
shouting the whole interior of the big cavern, of
which this was the entrance. Were the boys
asleep in some unexplored cavity? Well, as a
fact, they were not; but I must not anticipate.

H

CHAPTER XII.

SURPRISING EMPTINESS OF THE DEVIL'S PARLOUR.

THE murder was out. All was known. Thrusting the letter into my pocket, I rushed at the door like a madman, and, forgetting that I had locked it myself, thundered upon it with my fists, roaring, "Saddle Grey Franey!" It was the name of my fastest horse. "Saddle Grey Franey!" I continued to roar. The boys, who were all the time in the passage outside my door, clamoured in reply. One of them seemed to run off into the yard shrieking out my message. My wife and the servants came to the door of the office. In short, it seemed as if the whole household had gone suddenly mad. Of course, what I describe here only took a few seconds to pass.

I opened the door and rushed along the passage, not caring whom I threw down, through the kitchen, out into the yard, and straight to

the stable I ran. There already my orderly and
Joseph, working as for life and death, were
saddling and bridling Grey Francy. In another
moment I was on his back, without my hat,
tearing down the avenue, and then along the
road which led to the Rectory. I was aware of
people standing here and there with scared faces,
but little I cared for that.

Since I was born, I was never so mad as that
day, nor if I live for a thousand years could I
be so again. I took Franey at a leap over the
avenue gate of the Rectory, and galloped up to
the house, shouting as I did so, "They are
found!" The avenue is a short one. My
voice could have been heard from the gate in
every room of the house, and was. No com-
mander in the hottest moment of battle ever
roared to his men as I did that day, as I galloped
up to Mr. Freeman's hall door. Everyone there
knew the significance of my wild shoutings.
"They are found!" could refer only to the
two lost ones. Mrs. Freeman rushed from the
hall door before I reached it. She raised her

H 2

hands to the sky, as if in prayer, then sank on her knees and fell forward. The boy Charley came after and then the servants. After all came Mr. Freeman, his face as white as paper, but his manner calm and collected. Through the wood and shrubbery several men came rushing and tumbling, and behind me up the avenue others who had followed me along the road.

In a few words I told Mr. Freeman all. "Have you the letter?" he said. When I showed it to him he looked down first at the signatures, then read the letter, and handed it back to me without a word; but the look that was in his face what pen could interpret? Certainly not mine. I did not wait an instant longer, but galloped back straight to my own house. I had recovered my self-possession. On the way I met the boys and the orderly, and after that three of my men wearing their usual cast iron expression, and striding quietly in the direction taken by their insane officer. Indeed I am much too excitable to command a force whose gravity would put the Spaniard to shame.

As it was now drawing towards dusk, and various preparations and arrangements had to be made, I postponed the descent till next morning. I procured ropes that night from the village. I sent for a man, now a farm-labourer in the neighbourhood, but who I knew had formerly worked in mines in Cornwall, and consulted him about the best means of descent. He went from me to the forge of the village blacksmith, who under his directions made that night a sort of iron stirrup to be attached to the rope's end. I set the boys to make torches of splintered bog-wood. Harry, however, who was ingenious, provided besides sods of turf soaked in paraffin oil. These stuck on the ends of spits, he assured me, would make a grand blaze. We tried one and found it excellent.

The news flew like wild-fire over the country, and those who held by the *piast* theory were put to shame. Crowds of people came about the house, till the nuisance reached such dimensions that I ordered my men to clear them away, which they did with difficulty.

The public-houses in Dunbeacon were full that night, and the publicans did a roaring trade. I nominated the men who were to proceed with me in the morning to the Devil's Parlour, ordered them to be in readiness an hour before dawn, and strictly commanded them to tell no one.

I did not go to bed at all that night, though I may have dozed a little by the office fire. At five I woke up the boys. At six my party—and none but my party—being assembled, we started, well provided with strong ropes, candles, torches, paraffin-steeped turves, lucifer matches, etc. I had with me, too, a flask of brandy and sandwiches. I did not know in what exhausted condition I might find the lost ones.

It was quite plain now that from the cleft called the Devil's Parlour there were two ways leading down—one a blind alley ending in the small chamber, the same that had been explored by Edward Freeman, the other, which was the true entrance, conducting into some great subterranean cavern, to which there were two openings—one here on the hillside, the other the square opening in the sea-cliff, viz., the hole out of which Crohoor-beg's imaginary *piast* had projected itself in that very remarkable and terrible manner, when she devoured the Lan-beg men.

Arrived at the spot we finished our preparations and waited for the light, for it was still dark. It was not raining, but the weather was wild, and a strong gale blew from the west. I bade a man who had been with Edward Freeman show me the place where he had made the descent. Avoiding this, I put my foot in the stirrup and bade them lower away. I had round my neck, fastened by a strap, a bag containing half a dozen of Harry's peculiar torches, and in my hands, which clasped both it and the rope, a long spit to serve as a handle for those torches. For a short time I had to keep myself away from the rock with my second foot, that which was not in the stirrup. Presently I felt myself swinging in mid-air and in black darkness, and certainly in some vast hollow. In a few minutes more I should be clasping the hands of the poor lost lads.

Then I shouted. Vast hollow echoes and reverberations, travelling through what seemed interminable spaces of endless galleries, responded to my shout—echoes and reverberations, and nothing else. That surprised me, but did not much surprise me. The cavern was plainly enormous, and there were far-away winding corridors into which my voice might not travel. Moreover, the boys might be, and probably were, asleep.

"We will soon find them and wake them up," I said.

I continued at intervals to shout "Jack!" "Ned!" and as loudly as I could roar. Still there came no response but the huge echoes, which now sounded in my ears like the laughter and mockery of subterranean giants. Whether I was descending or not I could not tell. Above me it was as dark as below, and of course I had long since ceased to hear the voices of those at the cave's mouth, and the running of the rope over the block of timber which my miner had laid on the edge of the precipice. No doubt I

was descending, but for all I could feel or perceive I might be fixed and stationary in the
darkness or even ascending.

The minutes now began to seem like hours.
Should I ever reach the bottom of this awful
abyss? And to think that those pleasant young
friends of mine, so gay, bright, and good-
natured, so full of life, vigour, and activity,
should be immured here—one of them for many
months! Again and again I shouted: "Jack!
Ned! Ned! Jack! Are you there? Hullo!
hullo!" and still no sound reached my ears but
the mocking laughter of the huge, gaunt, and
supernatural echoes, which seemed to grow
greater as I descended, and rolled like thunder
round the cavern.

At last I heard a sharp click under my feet
and experienced a soft shock. I was on the
bottom. The click was the noise of my iron
stirrup striking on rock or stone. Still keeping
my foot in the stirrup, I threw off my bag of
turves, opened it, stuck one on the point of
my spit, struck a match, and ignited the

torch.   It sent out a great blaze, but revealed,
where I stood, nothing but great boulders, and
on one side the walls of the cavern, rising sheer
and black.

I gave the preconcerted signal—two strong
jerks at the rope—which was at once drawn
up.   The rope and stirrup looked very curious
dangling there above my head as they disappeared into the thick and black darkness.   I
continued to shout at intervals, but eventually
desisted until the coming of my assistants.
Either the Freemans were sound asleep, or were
in some far gallery of the cavern beyond the
reach of my voice; or they were now—terrible
thought!—beyond the reach of human help,
and we were too late—perhaps only a few hours
too late.

The next to descend was my head constable;
then, in succession, the two boys, Harry and
Joseph, then my orderly, and last, a sub-constable named Mulvaney, the same who formerly
went down into Curry's Window.   These and
no more I had permitted to descend.   I bade

"IT SENT OUT A GREAT BLAZE" (*p.* 106).

the orderly remain with the rope and keep his
torch burning there. All together now we raised
our voices and shouted as loud as we could bawl,
and did so again and again.

Save the echoes, now grown more vast and
appalling, there was no response. I was becoming more and more alarmed. If the boys
were alive they must have heard that shout.
The part of the cavern in which we found ourselves seemed to be a long and not very wide
gallery. We explored this to the end, and, as
we had plenty of torches, the whole floor of the
gallery was brilliantly illuminated. Not a thing
out of the common could escape our notice here.

Strewn on the floor were several of poor
Charley's cakes. We came to the end of this
gallery, turned back, passed the orderly where
he stood beside the rope with his torch burning
in his hand, and after a while found ourselves in
a much vaster space, the roof of which even the
combined light of our torches did not reveal at
all.

On one side of this space there was a pool of

agitated water, to which the floor of the cavern sloped rapidly. In its vicinity, and running somewhat in the same direction as that which we had already explored, ran another great gallery, the roof of which we could see. This also we now explored yard by yard, scrutinising the floor carefully as we went. Unlike the other, which ended in a mere wall of rock, this gallery ended in a great pool or pit of madly-boiling water.

We returned to that great central space from which these galleries branched, and explored it foot by foot. Here we made the first discovery. It was my nephew, Harry, who made it—viz., traces of a fire. On a level rock, not only were there all the signs of a hearth, but in its vicinity an enormous heap of ashes.

It was plain that this fire had been burning many months. After the excitement which attended this discovery, and the consultation which succeeded it, we moved forward. In short, we explored step by step and foot by foot every portion of the cave up to the entrance in the sea-cliff, by which they had come in, without finding the lost ones. We discovered many traces of them—bones of the sheep from which the bladder had been extracted, crumbs of bread near that hearth-place, and other signs and tokens, but alive or dead the Freemans were not there.

We learned, too, how they had been trapped —how, having got in, they were unable to get out again; and also indications of their pathetic efforts to climb out of their trap. Many signs and tokens of the recent presence of the brothers, and especially of the long-continued residence there of poor John Freeman, we found there, but not what we wanted to find—themselves. Again and again we searched the vast cavern through and through, expecting now only to find their bodies sunk in some cleft of the great boulders with which the cavern seemed filled, but our search was vain.

As our investigations became closer and more minute, we discovered various other relics and signs of the presence of the brothers, but neither their bodies nor any opening into which they might have fallen.

True, they might have died on the edge of that pool, which evidently communicated with the sea by some passage, for the water there ebbed and flowed; they might have died on its verge, and their bodies might afterwards have been floated away on the rising tide and borne through that passage.

Again, they might have committed suicide by throwing themselves into that boiling chasm in which the second of those galleries I have referred to terminated—a chasm like a huge cauldron of madly-seething waters. Yet there was something incredible and quite absurd in both theories. When they wrote that letter and signed it, they were in good health and had plenty of food. That they had plenty of food we knew as well from their letter as from its presence in the cavern, for, besides Charley's cakes, we discovered their storehouse—a cranny between two boulders—in which were bread and pieces of salted mutton. It was easy to see, too, how that mutton had been procured. Hard by were the bones of a sheep, from which the flesh had been stripped.

The sheep had evidently been " clifted," to use a local expression—that is to say, had fallen from above through the opening into the cavern. We did not disturb that little magazine. Indeed, we added to it, leaving there the whole supply of sandwiches which I had brought with me for the use of my party. The flask of brandy I laid there too. The whole affair of the disappearance of the brothers was so extraordinary and surprising, I believed it might eventuate in new and still more extraordinary developments. In presence of this mystery I could now believe in anything. I will not trouble you with an account of our consultations, theories, and guesses. Enough to say that after having spent six or seven hours in that cavern we came up again into daylight, not wiser but sadder men.

By this time a huge crowd of people was assembled on the hill-side—Mr. and Mrs. Freeman, Sam, and the little boy Charley amongst them. I was the last to ascend. I hoped that they might have taken their departure before my arrival, but they had not, and I had the misery—and intense misery it was—to explain to them the nature and extent of our explorations and our vain discoveries. I shall never forget the faces of the bereaved parents as I communicated the melancholy tidings.

Mr. Freeman, myself, and the orderly now made the descent. Little Charley, whose narrative stands at the head of this story, and his elder brother Sam, were not permitted to go down. I took Mr. Freeman through the vast cavern and showed him everything. His self-command was extraordinary. His face was pale and rigid, but not another sign of grief was apparent. When he spoke the tones of his voice were low and quiet. There was nothing new to be seen or inferred. At length we all returned to the upper air.

As I was parting from the Freeman party the little boy Charley tugged me by the coat. " What is it, Charley ? " I said.

"I am glad you left those things in their storehouse," he answered. "Something told you they are there still, and alive. Something tells me the same."

I started and looked at him, but turned again at once and walked away. Something had not told me they were there; yet, indeed, if I had not deposited the basket of sandwiches in that cranny to be eaten by the lost brothers, and that flask of brandy to be drunk by them, why did I leave those things? The little boy was right before. He knew that his brother John was at the bottom of the Devil's Parlour. Might he not be right now? I turned round once more. He was standing in the same place looking after me. His parents were now at some distance — Mrs. Freeman leaning heavily on the arm of her husband, and apparently weeping.

"I shall try again, Charley," I called out. He nodded approvingly, and darted away after his parents with an animation and cheerfulness which surprised me. "Out of the mouth of

I

babes and sucklings," I murmured to myself as I walked home.

Later on the same evening I had a singular interview with the singular boy called Sam. I was strolling along a boreen near the Rectory in the dusk, smoking and meditating, when I saw Sam coming towards me. He had a bundle of rabbits slung over one shoulder, and in his hand carried a string of blackbirds, redwings, field-fares, and such-like small deer, for he is a most industrious and successful trapper and maker and setter of the engines which we call "cribs." He was going past me, when I stopped him.

"Why don't you speak to me, Sam?" I said.

"You brought a lot of fellows down this morning, and you never asked me," he answered.

"Well, I am sorry for that, Sam; but you shall go down the next time."

This seemed to mollify him, but he answered, to my surprise, "I don't think I shall go."

"Why?" said I.

"Because I think we're all making a great deal too much fuss about those fellows. When they're tired of being away they'll come home. You don't know them as well as I do. They're both a little cracked." This was a long speech for Sam.

"And Charley?" said I.

He stopped and looked at me, but said nothing. I guessed what his thoughts were. He plainly regarded Charley as a prophet, seer, or something of that sort.

"Send me word when you are going down," he said, after a short delay, and so stepped through the hedge and took a short way home.

I sat up all that night strictly by myself, pondering the extraordinary events of the day. It is now daylight. I have spent the last four hours in writing the official account and this private one. Farewell.

CHAPTER XIII.

"December 23.

" I HAVE just returned from a second exploration of this mysterious cavern, as close and as minute as the first. The loaves which Charley Freeman threw down recently have not been touched, nor the articles which I placed in the cranny. Saw a seal in one of the pools. Perceive now how they contrived to send out their letter. I am almost mad with excitement.

"SAMUEL WATKINS."

(Same to same—written in pencil.)

"December 24.

" Have explored the cave for the third time. The flask is gone ; the sandwich basket opened ; some of the contents eaten or taken away. No sign of the brothers. I am confounded. I have left men in the cavern, and shall keep them there in permanence. The suspense is

terrible. I am returning to the cave myself.
Send this after post-car by orderly.

"SAMUEL WATKINS."

(Same to same, also in pencil marks.)

"December 24.

"FOUND!!!

"Harry has just run in to say so, and I hear
the people shouting.—S. W."

CHAPTER XIV.

EDWARD FREEMAN'S NARRATIVE (*continued*).—
EDWARD FREEMAN LOSES HIMSELF, BUT FINDS HIS
BROTHER.

THE preservation of my brother's life, in the first
instance, and his final escape from his place of
imprisonment, were both due—as I often heard
my father assert, and as both Jack and myself
also believe—to the grace of God, and not the
wisdom of man. The police and the coastguards were quite at a loss all through, and could
do nothing. Even the clever detective who
came from Dublin and spent a fortnight here
observing and considering, went away again in a
sort of passion. It was the extraordinary vision
seen by my little brother Charley that led him
to roll loaves into the place where Jack was really
imprisoned, and so perhaps saved his life.
Finally I myself found out the secret of his

imprisonment not by any wise calculation, but from a sort of inspiration which came to me quite unsolicited.

One day — shall I ever forget it? — a whimsical thought, but really a prompting of Providence, came into my mind. It was just before breakfast, and as I sat balancing a spoon on the edge of a tea-cup and thinking about Jack. Might not something happen, or some idea strike me, if I were to go to Du-Corrig fishing, just as my brother did? When I lost an arrow I used to come back to the spot whence I shot it and shoot another in the same direction and with equal force in order to find the first. It was this that put me in mind of the plan I was now about to execute.

I said nothing about it to anyone, but taking my rod set off for Du-Corrig. I fished carelessly, or pretended to fish, for some time. Then I got tired. "This," I said, "is perhaps how Jack felt six months ago. Fish not taking, nothing to do; I will try another rock; but

there are none here on the right, only the sheer
wall of cliff—try leftwards then." I clambered
along here till I came to a deep fissure in the
cliff-side. It ran sheer down to the sea—really
a rather horrible chasm, or long and profound
cleft, at the bottom of which the sullen waters
seemed talking to themselves.

I had already explored this cavern by sea in
my far-extended searches for Jack, having sculled
a boat through it from end to end, for it was too
narrow for rowing. I was on the point of turning back, for it never occurred to me that any
one would be so mad as to try and cross it.
Where I now stood it was too wide to leap
across, but as I looked up and down, I saw a
place where an active leaper, gifted with a good
deal of nerve, or rather afflicted with a sudden
attack of lunacy, might leap over it. The cleft
was not indeed so very wide at this point, but
the narrowness of the foot-hold at the other
side, and the darkness and depth of the abyss
below, brought the consequences of failure
before the imagination in a somewhat appalling

manner. Moreover, beyond that little foot-hold there seemed nothing but the sheer cliff.

Still keeping my rod in my hand I leaped it, right glad to find that my foot did not slip on the narrow, sloping ledge at the other side. Just then the conviction started suddenly into my mind that I was on Jack's traces. My heart beat so that I could hear it, and I had to stand still for a considerable time before its beatings and my general agitation would allow me to go on. I was now on the side of an almost sheer cliff, one which when seen from the water seemed quite sheer and untraversable; but I found a little ragged ledge leading onward and upward. One part of it was very dangerous, but after passing this I came upon rough craggy ground, quite easy to get over. This rough way led steadily upwards along the face of the cliff; by it alone was the rock traversable, and it was not wide. If Jack came along this cliff at all I should now find him or his body. I went on and on for nearly a mile—the little ledge being always traversable—and at last, quite

suddenly, arrived at a black opening in the
face of the cliff, which I had never noticed
before.

I may add that, unlike Jack, I did not care
for sea-fishing, was seldom on the water, and had
never scanned our cliffs with his hawk's eye and
inquiring mind. As I stood in the mouth of
this cave I was too filled with hope and fear to
cry out. I stood there on the flat sill for a
long time. Then I heard the sound of feet, as
if someone was stepping briskly over rocks, and
even springing actively from one to another,
though all was dark within. Then a cheery
whistle sounded in the interior. The air was
" Vilikins and His Dinah." Well I knew who
whistled. It was either Jack or his ghost.
There was a smooth incline of rock sloping
inwards just in front of me. Crying out I know
not what, I slid, or even cast myself, down this
incline.

I heard Jack roar at me to stay back, but I
could not, for the incline rapidly grew steeper,
till at last it was nearly sheer. So I came

tumbling down, and fell and rolled over something soft. In a moment I was on my feet again, and found myself in my brother's arms. I think we must have both cried aloud, weeping for joy. Certainly neither of us could speak for a long time.

As soon as we recovered ourselves Jack brought me round his vast domain, relating all his history as we went, while I told him all that had happened in the outer world.

Though I too was now trapped and a prisoner, I did not mind it in the least.

I was surprised and delighted with all I saw: Jack's tame seals; his fire burning so mysteriously in the huge darkness; the reflections on the rock-walls of the prison and on the Seals' Pool; the enormous echoing corridors of the cavern; the great central space where he had taken up his abode; two galleries—

[Here I must cut short Edward Freeman's narrative and invite the reader's attention to John Freeman's account of all his adventures and of what he had endured and dared in this great underground prison. We must, of course, to fully unravel the details, go back to the beginning, that is, to the day of John Freeman's mysterious disappearance.—EDITOR.]

CHAPTER XV.

[So far as the reader is concerned there is an end
now of the mystery. Henceforth for a good
while we shall be concerned only with John
Freeman's account of the extraordinary shifts
and lucky accidents by which he contrived not
only to remain alive in this cave for so many
months, but to retain his health and spirits to
such a degree that when his brother Edward at
last hit upon him, in the manner just described,
he was whistling lustily, and was plainly in no
way discouraged or cast down. For myself, I
can say that I have been far more deeply
interested in Mr. John Freeman's account of his
life in the cavern than in any other portion of
the whole story.—EDITOR.]

It was half-past three when I reached Du-
Corrig. I fished for a good while without even

a bite. A boat, which was locally known as "the old rake," rowed past me. The men in it were going to a noted "bream-rough" some miles further up the coast. I hailed them as they passed. I continued fishing for about half an hour after this without success. Then I wearied of the task, and began to cast about for something to do till sunset, at which time the pollock would begin to take—a fish that gives good sport. I thought of exploring the cliffs which lay eastward from Du-Corrig. When last I had clambered along these cliffs I was stopped by a gap across which I feared to spring lest I should not be able to return. That was two summers since, and I wished to see whether it looked as formidable to me now as it did then.

The only real object of interest in these cliffs was a small square aperture at a great height from the water. I had often noticed this aperture, which from the sea looked only a little square black spot. No one in the neighbourhood knew anything about it. But once, while out with an ancient fisherman from an adjoining island, I was told by him that it was the mouth of a haunted cave, and that it was unlucky to have anything to do with it. Indeed, it was difficult to see how a person could come at it at all, for it was quite unattainable from the sea or from any other side, so sheer and smooth seemed the cliff in which it was situated. This old fisherman called it "Curry's Window," and spoke of Curry as a great smuggler. Curry, he said, was so active that he would take a barrel of rum under one arm and a barrel of rum under the other, and, though weighted so, spring from the deck of his schooner and fly clean through the aperture into the cave.

When I made some chaffing remark about the old smuggler's extraordinary activity, he only said that Curry was known to be "a clever man," and no more would he say. I asked about Curry on another occasion, but he not only refused to add anything, but rather angrily denied that he had ever spoken to me about Curry at all. All this naturally excited my curiosity. Knowing that I was much bigger

and stronger than when I last made the
attempt, I resolved to try again. I easily
reached the gap to which I refer. Here there
was a split in the cliff reaching down to the sea.
Far below in the darkness the sullen waters were
murmuring. At the other side there was a good
foothold, but it was decidedly lower than the
point from which one would have to spring in
order to reach it; consequently the return leap
would be more difficult, and it was this as well
as the horrible depths below and the gulping and
gurgling of the dark waters which had daunted
me before. I perceived now that it was really
no such wonderful leap after all, and surprised at
my poltroonery on the former occasion, I sprang
over, and then sprang back again with com-
parative ease. After this proof of my prowess
I resolved to forego the rest of the exploration
till next day, intending to bring my brother
Ned with me. Though two years younger he
was a better leaper than myself, being slight
and long-legged, whereas I was made rather
for strength than activity. My evil genius,

however led me on, and the thought of the two hours yet wanting till sunset and the time when pollock would begin to rise.

The exploration did not indeed promise much, for the cliff as seen from Du-Corrig, as well as from the sea, seemed one sheer unbroken wall of rock, apparently offering no foothold to any creature less prehensile than a fly, yet immediately before me there was a very narrow traversable ledge. In traversing this I saw it would be an advantage to have my rod with me in order to steady my footsteps.

I returned for it to Du-Corrig, and a third time cleared the chasm, and presently encountered a piece of cliff-walking which could not possibly have been managed without such aid. There was a ledge, indeed, but the cliff above it was so sheer, or rather inclined forward so much, that some slight support for the climber on the seaward side was necessary in order to get along here. The iron spike at the end of the rod supplied a good rest for me as I went.

J

Passing this dangerous point I was delighted
to find that the cliff was still traversable, though
with difficulty, and I had frequently to crawl.
Yet I continued to get forwards and also upwards. In this manner I progressed about a
mile, not knowing whither that traversable
ragged ledge led me, but hoping it might be to
Curry's Window. As my progress was slow I
should upon ordinary evenings have been perceived by some passing boat, but the people
were at this time very busy about hay, and "the
old rake" was the only one which, on this
unlucky evening, had put forth from our little
harbour, "the Basin," as we used to call it.
Eventually I found myself all of a sudden
looking into a considerable cave in the cliff side
—Curry's Window, as I plainly perceived. I
was surprised to find it so large, and also that it
was not square, but irregularly arched. I used
to think that the famous smuggler would have
found a difficulty in rolling even one barrel at a
time through the aperture.

The delusive appearance of perfect squareness

had, of course, been caused by distance, for the aperture was very high up in the cliff. It, however, resembled a window in this respect, that the sill, so to speak, was perfectly smooth, flat, and horizontal, as if the work of man's hands. The rest of the aperture was very jagged and ragged. I also saw that the rock on the inside was smooth, and sloped away from the sill, gently at first, but afterwards at an angle of forty-five degrees, or thereabouts. The sun had now got round the shoulder of the hill, whose base was supplied by these cliffs; consequently I could see little or nothing of the interior of the cave, but thought that I could perceive the bottom at a short distance. I pushed the butt end of the fishing rod before me, and found that this was so. There, about six feet below me, was the bottom of the incline, and apparently the floor of the cave.

CHAPTER XVI.

TRAPPED.

I sat on the edge of the sill and slid down, expecting to land safely on the spot which I had poled and probed with the butt end of my rod, but it proved to be a false bottom, or not the bottom at all. Whatever was the obstruction at this point, it gave way before my descending weight. It was, in fact, an accumulation of *débris* gathered around certain rotten branches that had stuck here in the entrance, lying transversely along the incline. I broke through all this with a loud crackling of broken timber, and continued to slide—or, indeed, rush—down a still steeper incline descending into the darkness; and when I believed that I was being precipitated into eternity, fell into a soft mass of what seemed dry sea-weed, without sustaining any injury.

" *Facilis descensus*," I cried, as I landed on

"IT GAVE WAY BEFORE MY DESCENDING WEIGHT" (*p.* 1,2).

this soft bed, all my alarm yielding suddenly to a sense of the ridiculous. Seeing the window at such a moderate distance above my head, I had not the least doubt that, even if the slope should prove too sheer, I could easily swarm or clamber up at the point where this slope met the walls of the cave.

The moment I found my feet I was bent all on exploration. I struck a match, and by its transient and faint light sought to inspect the fabulous smuggler's storehouse. I continued to light one match after another. Eventually gathering all the remainder in a little bundle, I ignited them, in order that by their united blaze I might see as much as was possible under the circumstances.

When they had burned out, and I had thrown away the stumps and had seen almost nothing, I bethought me of the return journey, and also that it would be better to make haste, for it would be ill work groping my way home in the dark along the face of that sheer cliff. I tried to swarm up the incline, but failed. Now a comical thought entered my mind. I thought of a cockroach in a glass trap, and laughed. I had often watched, with some faint glimmerings of pity and compunction, the futile efforts of these black gentry to climb the smooth sides of their prison. My own futile efforts to climb the slope suggested a ludicrous resemblance to the frustrated energies of those insects. Again and again I addressed myself to different parts of the smooth slope, but nowhere could secure a purchase for hands or knees. I was not yet alarmed—yet, as if far down in the depths of my nature, I was conscious of a dim, formless emotion, which I never experienced before.

Still, certain that I should in some way escape, I sought the point where the incline abutted on the wall of the cave, sure that I could get up in the angle so formed; and by the support of the craggy sides there. I tried first on the left. Here, however, the incline seemed to break off sharp. I found this out, of course, by my sense of touch, for I could hardly see anything. Then, creeping ·over huge smooth boulders and the aforesaid heap of sea-weed, I reached the other wall and found it ragged indeed and abutting on the incline, but at this point the incline was almost sheer. In short, I could not ascend.

Despair was now fast getting the upper hand in my mind. Nevertheless, I made frantic efforts to ascend, but all in vain. Again I thought of the cockroaches in the glass trap—the wretched insects clambering and sliding on the smooth wall of their prison. But I did not laugh this time. I was too like them. Yet I did not in the least despair of getting out—if not to-night, which was improbable, then to-morrow. I knew there were many devices to be tried yet. For one thing I thanked Heaven sincerely : the place where I fell was carpeted thick with sea-weed. On each side there was none. Whatever the gales or the crests of great waves in winter had thrown in had been washed down through the interstices of the great boulders, and probably escaped at some lower point in the cliff's sides. Had I not descended exactly in the middle I should certainly have been killed or maimed. I sat down on this providential sea-weed to collect my thoughts; I filled my pipe, and then searched all my pockets, hoping somewhere to discover a match, for I used to keep loose matches indifferently in all my pockets, and often had found one hid somewhere in the lining. My search was bootless, I had not a match left.

It was growing dark rapidly; I had no time to lose, for even if I were to effect my escape from this infernal cave, I would require daylight for the return journey along that dangerous cliff-road. I proceeded at once to gather together all the sea-weed that I could lay my hands on, and piled it up in a heap against the incline. As the heap rose my heart rose with it. There seemed an abundance of sea-weed: I could feel it thick under my feet. Its crackling sounded pleasantly, for it was very dry. Still, I had to go further and further into the cave for each armful, or *barth*, to use a local word, for it did not lie everywhere, but, as it were, in a line running inward from the middle of the incline. Here lay a road of sea-weed a few feet wide, but on either hand only bare stone.

It was now getting so dark that I at last determined to give over this labour, for it would be sheer madness to attempt the return journey in the night. A sinister suspicion, too, was growing in my mind that the supply of sea-weed was giving out. My last armfuls represented a good deal of groping. The sea-weed only seemed to be really abundant close under the window. I did not wish to make my suspicion a certainty by putting the facts to too close a test. The thought of the anxiety and alarm of my parents and family, as may be imagined, contributed a good deal to my unhappiness. When I ceased working I began to grow cold, and soon very cold. The sea-weed was quite dry and crisp; I piled a great deal of this over me by way of bed-clothes, and, thanks to youth and health, ere long fell sound asleep in spite of my troubles.

When I awoke it was broad daylight, and

the level rays of the sun streamed far into the
interior of the cave, which seemed of vast extent.
Indeed, I guessed as much on the previous night
as I listened to the reverberations of my voice in
its abysmal hollows. Starting up, I at once
renewed my task of collecting sea-weed with the
object of ascending the incline by its aid.

"*Facilis descensus*," I had cried merrily
enough after my tumble last night, but ere
long the rest of the quotation continued to
haunt me, viz :—

> "Sed revocare gradum superasque evadere ad auras,
>   Hoc labor, hoc opus."

CHAPTER XVII.

NOT TO GET OUT.

PRESENTLY I found that I had already collected nearly all the sea-weed that was procurable at this end of the cave. But after my first sense of disappointment I did not so much mind this, for I expected to meet with plenty of stones, such as one often finds in the interior of such caves. All such pebbles, however, as I could see seemed much too large to lift. But I did not doubt that I could somewhere find removable pebbles in sufficient quantity to build up for myself a sort of scaling ladder against the mouth of my prison. Yet I went to the extreme limit of the daylight without finding such, and afterwards, penetrating the sheer darkness, groped about in all directions without success. Everywhere I scrambled only over large boulders. Still groping forward in the darkness, urged now by the fury of despair, I found myself suddenly cut off altogether from even a view of the window. I had gone round some angle of rock, and was immersed in dense darkness.

I gave myself up for lost, and having searched around in vain without perceiving anywhere a ray of light, sat down and—well, not to be too proud—wept long and bitterly. Then, praying fervently, and thinking with such feelings as may be imagined of the opening line of that little familiar collect, "Lighten our darkness, we beseech thee, O Lord," which I had so often repeated with little or no thought of its meaning, and which was now naturally brought to my remembrance, I searched again for the light, clambering recklessly over the boulders, and at length, to my extreme joy, perceived a faint ray.

Moving towards it, I suddenly caught sight of Curry's Window, and, however I might have been inclined to curse that sinister aperture, now sincerely blessed it, and the level rays which shot through it into the inner gloom. I thought of Milton's line, "Hail! holy Light, offspring of Heaven first born." I may mention here that I was very fond of poetry, and had stored away a great deal of it in my memory, so that I could repeat a vast number of the English lyrics, and even long passages from Spenser, Shakespeare, and Milton. This intellectual provision or accomplishment, or whatever it may be called, proved a great blessing to me in my miserable imprisonment, and was probably the means, under Providence, of preserving my reason.

With the rediscovery of Heaven's blessed light, hope revived—hope, and also hunger. Now, for the first time, I thought of food, for, though nigh famished, I had not been quite conscious of it hitherto, owing to the feverish excitement into which I had been thrown. I had with me half a slice of bread, which, knowing that I would not be home till late, I had thrust into one of my pockets before starting for Du-Corrig. As for water, I was safe. Searching round the walls of my prison the previous night, I found the rock upon the

right side slippery from wetness, and at one
point felt water running against my fingers.
Also, in the interior somewhere, I heard, though
far away, the plash of descending water. I ate
my bread and, going to the spot where I had
felt moving water on the previous night, made a
cup with my hand, and pressing the inside edge
of it against the rock, and doing this again and
again, got a good drink of very pure spring
water. I now resolved to search the cave more
carefully than I had done before for pebbles
such as I could remove, and to be particularly
cautious about losing sight of the window.

I searched around now for hours, but in
vain. Hardly a stone of the kind could I
discover. I returned to my bed of seaweed
and lay down to rest. I was now painfully
conscious of growing weakness. My excitement
was wearing away, and the lack of food
beginning to tell. It was now about midday.
From time to time I shouted as loudly as I
could, but only heard for response the mocking
echoes and reverberations of my own voice.

Knowing that boats were not likely to be passing in the middle of the day, I determined to husband my energies in this direction until the evening.

It was now certain that I could not climb out of my prison, or within the limits and vicinity of the light procure sea-weed or stones in sufficient quantity to make for myself a scaling ladder. My last hope lay in my rod and line. I piled up all the sea-weed procurable, took off my clothes and laid them on the top of the heap, and thrusting upwards the butt end of the rod, endeavoured, by means of the crook supplied by the reel, to secure a purchase upon the sill of the window and so drag myself up out of this pit. If the rod and reel had only been strong enough, I might have succeeded. I was conscious that it was a forlorn hope, but, nevertheless, made the attempt. I did succeed in getting a grip somewhere at the sill with the reel, but, as soon as I began to climb, the top joint of the rod gave way, I tumbled down, rolled from the sea-weed heap on to the boulders, and was much bruised and shaken by the fall.

With the portion of the rod which remained in my hands I succeeded in disengaging the rest, which fell back into the cave. I next unreeled the line, doubled it, doubled it again, and made a pretty strong rope, which I fastened to the thicker part of the rod, and renewed my attempt, this time flinging up the rod and letting it slide back from the sill, hoping so that the reel, which was a large one, might catch. The rod and twisted line were indeed strong enough to bear my weight, but I had great difficulty on this occasion in securing a purchase with the reel, and, when I did, the moment my weight—which was considerable—fell upon the reel the shank went with a loud snap. Again I fell, and the reel tumbling after me rang on the boulders.

All was in vain. I had now tried every imaginable method of escape, and they had all failed. Evening was at hand, and the cave nearly black, even at the entrance, and I had grown horribly hungry; I had, however, plenty of pure water, and that was some comfort. I had some cut tobacco in my pouch, I had also a very large roll of what we used to call " Limerick Twist " in my fishing bag. I had bought it at a huckster's on my way to Du-Corrig, not for myself, but as a supply for the men who from time to time might be of service to me. It was the only form of reward that they would accept, ours being a primitive and unsophisticated neighbourhood. I had heard of some sort of comfort to be derived from the chewing of tobacco. I cut off a bit of the twist, and, after chewing it, felt my hunger abated, but also a disagreeable sense of vertigo accompanied with nausea. Nevertheless these sensations were a relief from the horrible feeling of utter prostration into which I was sinking. Eventually I fell asleep.

K

CHAPTER XVIII.

FIRE.

WHEN I awoke it was still night, but I felt the dawn approaching. I awoke extremely miserable, with a misery which my reflections on the nature of my dismal situation deepened almost into despair. I had now tried all conceivable devices of getting out of this horrible den, and I had eaten scarcely anything for thirty-six hours. I did not dare to pass beyond the precincts of the light in search of stones—my experience of being lost, as I had been yesterday, in the darkness, was too terrible. "If I am to perish," I said, "let me perish here in the light"—a sentiment which I know was expressed by someone else before me, I cannot now recall by whom, though I think I knew it then. Every device had failed. Nevertheless, as the light grew around me, I determined to make one more effort to escape by escalade. I successively attempted the two corners of the incline where it abutted on or approached the rock walls of my prison, but my efforts were still more futile than on the first occasion.

I was weak now, and strong only in weakness and misery. I drank a great deal of water this day. When night approached I was too miserable to sleep. I chewed and even swallowed some tobacco, but the succeeding nausea prevented me from doing so again. About midnight, I fancy, I drank water once more, and fell into a disturbed slumber, filled with abominable apparitions. When I awoke it was twilight, and most still, serene and beautiful about the faintly illuminated edges of the cave's mouth. I expected this day to be my last, and composed my thoughts to death as well as I could, and said my last prayers.

Nevertheless, the strong spirit of life seemed to flicker up within me again, and after I had taken a deep draught of water, I sat up on my sea-weed couch and searched all my pockets carefully for any stray crumb which might yet

K 2

linger there. Conveying anything that felt like
such to my mouth, I was aware of a certain
bitterish taste which I detected at once as that
of gunpowder. The old canvas jacket which I
wore on this occasion was that in which I used
to shoot when I was at home last winter for the
Christmas holidays. Some powder had escaped
from my powder-horn, I fancy. However the
powder got there, there it was, and immediately
the thought of procuring for myself light and
fire arose in my mind. Of timber I had plenty.
While handling the sea-weed I was conscious of
perpetually finding my fingers in contact with
bits of wood, swept in thither on the same crests
of storm billows which had brought the sea-
weed. Though it was still dark, I groped
around industriously, and ere long had collected
a considerable quantity of driftwood, large and
small, all exceedingly dry and brittle, and
some sheer touchwood, which crumbled in my
fingers.

Choosing a flat stone, I determined to make
it my hearth, and crumbled there a little heap of

the touchwood, making it as fine as dust, and
gathered to the same spot some of the very dry
timber which I had collected. Then I cut from
my trousers a scrap of the woollen cloth, and,
after wetting it, rubbed the gunpowder well into
its texture. As soon as I thought it was
sufficiently saturated I let it dry, but so eager
was I for the experiment that, to facilitate the
drying process, I fastened it to the point of
my rod, and held it up towards the opening
of the cave, that it might receive the sun's
rays.

When it seemed to be perfectly dry, I took it
to my hearth, and, unfolding my strong clasp-
knife, held the rag in my left hand, and with the
right, using the knife, I struck sparks from the
edge of a rock, making them fly on to the
powder-steeped rag. Finding it did not catch
fire, I put a little dry powder on the surface of
the rag, and renewed my efforts. I felt certain
of success, because at one time I used to shoot
with an old flint pistol which I had accidentally
discovered in my father's bureau, and therefore

knew how instantaneously such a flying spark
will ignite powder. At the second or third
stroke the powder blazed up with a puff and an
ascending cloud of smoke, and the rag began to
burn and crackle gaily. I laid it on the stone
and sprinkled lightly over it pinches of the
crumbled touchwood, and as this caught fire
sprinkled more in larger quantities, but still
gradually, knowing that too much fuel would
quench the fire. Then I poured on touchwood
less finely broken, and as soon as the glowing
mass seemed large enough, breathed upon it
gently, and soon had the satisfaction of seeing it
burst into a bright flame.

My delight can be imagined. I had now the
means of exploring the whole cave, and of
utilising all its resources, such as they might be,
for the purposes of escape or for food, if haply
anything in the nature of food might be procured there anywhere. Food, indeed, had now
become an absolute necessity if I was not to die.
I removed a bundle of my collected driftwood to
a distant point in the interior, and made another

fire there, and, taking good care not to lose sight
of this, proceeded to search all around for stones
such as I could remove, but found none anywhere, only large boulders, and in one place the
hard, bare bed of the cave, which here began to
slope downwards, not sheer, or at a dangerous
angle, but very decidedly downwards. I also
found a sort of pocket in the side of the cave,
a cave within a cave, which was filled with old
timber all very dry and brittle. Here the cavern
seemed to wind and curve leftwards. I made
another fire at the curve and passed onwards.
Henceforward there was nothing but the hard
rock bed of the cave. Indeed, it was too steep
for any boulders to rest here. Lighting one
more fire, I discovered a thin rivulet of water
falling from the roof or side of the cave, a slender
straight pencil of water.

I returned easily along my line of fires to the
entrance, feeding them as I went. The drift-
wood burned so rapidly that I now determined
to partially wet the fresh timber which I laid on,
that it might burn more slowly.

Again I went back along my line of fires, examining carefully the wall formation of the cavern, so that even if any of the fires went out I should be able to find my way back to the entrance and the daylight. And yet Curry's Window, as I could not ascend to it, was as cheerless as any other part of the cave.

My last interior fire was at the point where the floor of the cavern sloped so rapidly downwards. I hastened forward now with no thought but that of food—food—no matter what. By this downward way I descended so low that I suspected I must be on a level with the sea. Finding that the light of my last fire seemed faint and dim, I lit another in a dry spot, which was not easy to find, for the ground here was very damp and slippery owing to droppings from the roof. I then listened, hoping that I might hear the noise of the sea, for I thought that by some cleft the outer water might penetrate here. If that were so, I might get shell-fish, mussels, or limpets, or edible sea-weed, *myvane*, or *dilisk*, or *sloucane,** all edible weeds whose botanical names even now I do not know. My thoughts were so low and humble that they were concentrated chiefly upon sea-weed; for, edible or not, any live sea-weed would be edible to me.

* This weed is known in the London markets as " lever," and is considered a delicacy by some.—EDITOR.

CHAPTER XIX.

NOT A DOG SPITE ITS BARKING.

I now stood and listened with ears which famine had rendered preternaturally acute, hoping that I might somewhere hear the sullen gurgle of water or the lapping of waves upon stone. I stood so a long time, then, waving a torch, I stepped rapidly forward. I had only advanced a few yards when I heard something which caused me to start so violently that the torch fell from my hands. It was not the noise of regurgitating water or lapping waves, but a cry —loud, clear, and distinct, echoing far and wide in the convolutions of the huge cave, a cry repeated in quick succession again and again, a cry, rather a mew, or a bark, resembling indeed both sounds, but the latter more than the former. I was in that condition in which fear can at any moment burst out into frantic terror, but I recovered myself in an instant.

The noise which I had heard was the
barking of a seal. I had not spent my boyhood
on this coast without having acquired that much
of sea-side knowledge. I knew that it was a
seal, and even a young seal. Yes, the tidal
water had here somewhere an entrance into the
cave. I went on in the direction of the noise,
and was about to extinguish the burning timber
which I held in my hand when the increased
energy and frequency of the barking convinced
me that the seal, so far from being terrified by the
light, seemed to like it, and, as I believed, was
endeavouring to approach it. I stood again listening, and could hear its flappings and shufflings.

Still going on I came rather suddenly within
view of the creature. The water, which I could
now see, was a good many yards behind it, and
already, mad with hunger, I could see and smell
chops and steaks of the little seal frizzling on
one of my fires, for of course I had determined
to lose no time about killing and eating this
animal which Providence had so unexpectedly
cast in my way.

But when I saw the poor creature, my sole fellow-occupant of the gloomy prison, still flapping and flopping towards me, and the pathetic look in its eyes—for the seal can look very pathetic—an involuntary feeling of compassion rose within me. It was not in the least afraid of me, even when I came close up to it, probably because it was so much pleased with the light. No doubt ere long famine would have driven out pity; a man "feeling all the vulture in his jaws" will eat anything. But at this moment the light of my torch fell on something shiny on the edge of the water. It was a good-sized salmon, just a little nibbled at about the neck and shoulders, As in a flash I perceived that this little moaning suppliant, whom a few minutes before I had been on the point of killing, might be the means of my preservation. This large fish was never killed by the small seal; it was killed by its parents and brought thither as food for their offspring. I would keep the child a close prisoner and compel the parents to feed both it and me.

The fishing line of which I had spoken I had with me still fastened to the rod. I unwound its twisted cords and fastened one end round the seal's neck with a knot that would not slip, and made the other end fast round the projecting corner of a boulder.

Then rejoicing, I bore away the salmon, which, cut into thick steaks, was soon frizzling and spluttering gaily in the fire which was nearest. I knew now so well the lie of this end of the cave that I had no fear about finding my way to Curry's Window whenever I should feel inclined. Having duly said grace, and more earnestly than ever before in my life, I fell to and made a hearty meal. The seal was all this time crying piteously. When I had ended I gave it a piece of the broiled salmon, which it seemed to like. I knew then that the little seal and I would become good friends, and I hoped ere long by similar means to become acquainted with its parents. So pleased was I by the sudden turn which things had taken in my favour that I became quite joyous and happy, whistled and sang gaily, and awoke distant echoes, for the cave was far larger than I have indicated, and was even of vast extent. Resolved for the present to make my home in the vicinity of my new friend, I returned to the entrance for the useful sea-weed which had hitherto been my bed. It was near sunset, so I continued to shout at intervals as loudly as I could, in hope of attracting the notice of some passing boat. This continued to be a practice with me for many days, but the distance was so great that none of the fishermen ever heard me.

CHAPTER XX.

FRIENDS MULTIPLY.

WHEN I returned with the sea-weed, which was
to be my bed, I saw in the faint light cast from
my fire two large objects beside the little seal;
they were the parents. There was one on each
side of the youngster. They were lowering and
raising their heads towards him, while he was
flapping vigorously and uttering little cries
of joy. It was a pretty scene, and I feared to
disturb it. I had often heard, though had not
myself noticed it, that these animals are very
susceptible to music, and will for miles follow a
ship in which a musical instrument is being
played. Accordingly I began to whistle in a
low tone a plaintive air. The moment I began,
however, the elder animals took the alarm,
flapped away down the sloping rock, tumbled
into the water, and disappeared; not, however,
before one of them had attempted to carry off

the youngster in its jaws, just as a bitch would a puppy. Seals, I may observe, give suck to their young just as animals do. My little friend had got beyond this stage, and was beginning to eat on its own account.

Now that the parents were alarmed for the sake of their offspring, I knew that they would not go far. I brightened my fire so as to illuminate somewhat the whole pool, lay down beside it upon my weedy couch, and continued to whistle. Presently, in a distant part of it, close beside a dark rift or aperture in the rock, I saw four round eyes, apparently watching me, and perfectly motionless. I continued whistling so at intervals for more than two hours, hardly making any perceptible motion, during which time the animals had so far dismissed their fear that I could see them swimming about the pool, and sometimes coming to the edge and resting there. I was particularly anxious to make friends with these animals, for I feared that in their alarm they might desert the youngster. Then, too, I knew that the little seal might

"I SAW FOUR ROUND EYES APPARENTLY WATCHING ME" (*p.* 160).

gnaw through his tether at any time, and make away, or that his parents might cut it for him.

Accordingly I now resolved to make the tether stronger. This, fortunately, I could do. The "nostle" of my line—viz., the part between the line proper and the hook—was of wire, and in my fly-book, which contained many sundries, I had a good roll of the same article.

As I feared, however, to approach the pool while the parents were there, I ceased whistling, and waited till the parents should disappear. Though I was in an agony of drowsiness, I contrived to keep myself awake, and at length had the satisfaction of seeing them one after the other dive through the cleft. Then I wound the wire strongly round the whole length of the tether, and also very close and firm round the loop which encircled the little animal's neck. My life, I felt, depended on the excellence of my workmanship, and I did not spare pains. Then I returned to my fire, and, after having covered up the burning embers deep in ashes, lay down,

L

and in an instant was fast asleep. I slept profoundly without a dream, even at the moment of waking. When I awoke I thought I was in my own bed, but, alas! the touch of the dry sea-weed quickly banished the thought. Very cautiously and gradually, and whistling low all the time, I revived the fire. When the light was sufficient, I could see the parents lying beside their offspring, and perfectly motionless. There, too, I gladly perceived fish. I contrived gradually to edge my way towards them, whistling all the time. Though they made slight motions of alarm, they did not flap off till I had come within half a dozen yards of them. I found near the little seal a white trout and a young pollock, injured only by the marks of teeth, and after petting and making much of my little friend, who testified his pleasure at seeing me with many cries and awkward little jumps, returned to my fire and cooked my breakfast. Of course, I had determined to make an exploration of the whole cavern, but did not dare to do so until I had first established perfectly friendly relations with the creatures upon whose presence my life depended. I perceived, that owing to the intelligence, and, I might almost say, humanity, of these amiable and interesting animals, this, though difficult, was only a work of time. Amid such surroundings they did not, I think, quite associate the thought of me with that of their great enemy, man.

I now began to regulate my life according to the time of day and night, and to keep myself related with the upper world by going to sleep at about ten o'clock. No one who has not known such solitude as mine can be aware how much society there is in a watch, and its friendly, scarce-audible ticking. The whole of that day, with the exception of the time that I spent taking exercise in the vicinity of Curry's Window and in the genial light of day, I devoted myself to making friendly advances to the seals. It was slower work than I expected, but at the end of the fifth day they allowed me to touch them and stroke down their smooth polls as I would a dog.

L 2

Next day as I approached them, still very cautiously, they uttered cries of joy and affection, and by the evening our relations were satisfactory in every respect. That day, having for some time perceived that the little seal was pining for the water, I let it flap thither, and holding the tether in my hand, sat for more than an hour watching its delighted gambols as it dived and rose there, romping with its parents in a manner that would have delighted the hardest heart. Every day after this I allowed it to indulge in the same amusement, even for several hours. I knew that this swimming exercise was necessary for its health.

Yet only half my work with the seals was now accomplished. The little seal might die, or the parents, finding it big and strong, therefore uninteresting, might neglect to bring it food. I resolved, therefore, to teach the parents to bring *me* food, and this I did. When one of them appeared on the edge of the pool with a fish in his mouth, I used to take it from him myself, make much of him, and stroke him, and whistle the air he seemed to like best for his special edification. Then I cut out a piece of the fish and gave it to the youngster, but always insisted upon the fish being first given to myself. Eventually they always did this of their own accord, and would even pass by the youngster and come flopping up the rock towards me with the fish in their mouths.

All this, as may be imagined, was a work of time, yet the whole business of training the seals took only a little more than three weeks. To begin with, the seals on this coast were by no means wild, for they were never hunted or fired upon. Then, as I have already suggested, they did not, in this illuminated cavern, quite identify me with the thought of the arch-enemy. In the third place, there was the little seal puppy as a link of amity between us.

CHAPTER XXI.

FURTHER EXPLORATIONS.

LIKE Robinson Crusoe, of whom I often thought, I kept an almanack. One of the largest and smoothest boulders was used by me for this purpose. Like him I made a stroke for each day, a long stroke for Sunday, and at the beginning of each month wrote its name, all, of course, with the point of my knife.

After I had accustomed the seals to my presence, though before I had taught them to bring me fish, I began to explore the remainder of the cavern, and in the same way as I had explored it from the window to the Seals' Pool, viz., by lighting a series of fires. A little beyond the pool I found that the cavern forked— one gallery, which was the smaller, terminating in another pool of unknown depth (I tried, but could not sound it), in which the tide rose and fell: a terrible and mournful place, which, after that sounding or trying to sound, I seldom afterwards visited. The other gallery was of huge extent, and ran far inland. When I first penetrated this gallery, I noticed at one point that the air seemed to be fresher than elsewhere, and could perceive a slight motion in the flame of my torch. This, of course, was evidence that somewhere here there was communication with the outer world. Though I scanned eagerly the roof of the cavern, I could perceive there no welcome slit of sky. Nevertheless, I felt sure that a way to the outer world existed at this point, though probably so winding as not to permit the access of light. Then, as I recalled the physical character of that outer world under which I was entombed, I remembered a cleft opening into a deep and horrible abyss, which had always possessed a fascination for myself and my younger brothers.

It was called "The Devil's Parlour," and many times we rolled down stones here and listened with awe-struck delight to their clashing and rattling as they went down into

subterranean depths.   I used to maintain that it
was bottomless, and penetrated into the centre
of the earth, because I never could hear the final
clash which told that the stone was at rest
below.   Then I searched around, and here, sure
enough, did find a variety of stones, cast down,
no doubt, by the hands of many boys at many
times.   Also I found many bones of animals—
goats and sheep, which from time to time
during past centuries had fallen thither while
they grazed carelessly on the edge of the abyss,
or had been driven into it by dogs or wolves.
"If only one such would fall in here now,"
I thought to myself ruefully, as my imagination
drew pleasing pictures of roast meat.   In truth,
I was becoming heartily tired of my fish diet,
which was beginning to affect my health, and
still more noticeably my strength.   I blazed
my way to the end of this gallery, the extreme
limit of my gloomy kingdom.   Here I made
a singular discovery.

Against the black wall of the cave there
stood on end a great white boulder, lozenge-

shaped—that is to say, somewhat flat and oblong. Examining this, I discovered upon it not only a variety of circles, but a curious engraving something like a bent bow, with straight strokes upon it on the concave side. I noticed, too, upon the edges a variety of scorings which travelled round the side of the slab that was hidden from view. Feeling all around, I came to one point where I could pass my hand between the slab and the rock. There was a hollow space behind—how large I could not tell, but apparently considerable.

As it was evident that this slab had been set up here by men's hands, and in order to block access to the cavity behind, I at once concluded that this well-protected pocket was a treasure-chamber, or perhaps a tomb.

I threw in some lighted timber, and flinging more upon the top of it and making a blaze, I applied my eye to the cavity. I saw an earthen crock about the size of a large flower-pot, filled with something which I could not distinguish, but did notice both there and elsewhere what looked like metal of some kind. Owing to the smoke which gathered rapidly, I saw nothing distinctly, and after a moment or two, owing to the same cause, saw nothing at all.

"This," I said, "is surely old Curry the smuggler's treasure-chamber. If I ever get alive out of this den I will come back with my brother Ned; together we will blast away this boulder, or contrive in some way to rifle the old villain's treasures."

I never suspected what a terrific part this tomb was about to play in my subsequent history.

I had not as yet at all yielded to despair. I had only postponed my efforts to escape until I should have established friendly relations with the creatures through whose industry and affection I was to get food.

CHAPTER XXII.

ANOTHER ATTEMPTED ESCALADE.

AFTER I had thoroughly explored the whole cavern and perceived that no other outlet of an available character existed, I commenced to draw every movable article which I could discover to Curry's Window—stones, gravel, débris of all kinds, bones, etc. I knew that the supply was utterly inadequate to enable me to mount to the aperture, but would make the attempt nevertheless. Of course it failed, but a certain portion of the incline was thus made ascendable, and this was something. The storms of the approaching winter might fling in sufficient drift-wood, boards, and even beams big enough to enable me to construct a ladder. This idea of a ladder was present in my mind almost from the moment that I entered my prison. The extreme brittleness of the timber, amongst which there was hardly a sound bit, had prevented me from making the attempt before. I now determined to utilise the skeletons of the sheep and goats for the purpose, and to unwind the tether of the young seal to supply fastening material, keeping only the wire for tether. On the day after I discovered those bones I set to work.

Many of them were too brittle to be of any use. Some were sound ; others, though too brittle or too small to be separately of sufficient strength to bear my weight, I bound together. Some of the fresher drift-wood I treated in the same manner. Though I knew that I neither had material enough nor twine enough I laboured on. With every round made I was coming nearer to my deliverance, yet I believed my fishing-rod could supply more material for the ladder than all the rest put together. Seeing that even by cutting up the rod my ladder would not be nearly long enough, I forbore to destroy the rod, knowing that I could do it at any time. It was well that I refrained.

Though I have not had occasion to mention the fact, yet, shortly after my imprisonment, I was aware that pigeons of the slate coloured variety common along this coast were in the habit of roosting somewhere in the cave. In the dusk of the evening I had often seen them as they whirred through the window and disappeared into the interior darkness. While I was engaged in taming the seals I had made a close exploration of the cavern with the hope of finding their roost, and at last discovered it.

Standing perfectly still in different parts of the cave and listening intently, I could at one point hear them making little sleepy noises, but at such a height above me that, though I kindled a considerable fire here, I could not see them. Now, however, shortly after that exploration of the long gallery, I heard similar noises at a different point, and seemingly proceeding from a spot much nearer to the floor of the cavern. Here with the aid of a torch I could see some half-dozen of them upon a

ledge, all very close together. Next day I
fastened a large conor-hook, from which I had
first filed away the barb, to the extremity of
my fishing-rod, and leaned the rod against the
ledge upon which they roosted. I then lit a
fire, such as would throw a faint light upon
the ledge, and lay down close to the rod.

Duly the pigeons arrived and took up their
night quarters. They looked at first a little
surprised, and kept peering about with their
little bright round eyes, but presently clustered
close together as their custom was, and seemed
to fall asleep. Indeed, they were by this time
pretty well used to the fires and lights of the
cavern. Cautiously grasping the rod with one
hand, and bringing the point of the hook over
the back of one of the sleepers, I drew the
rod down quickly yet gently, and had the satisfaction of knowing that my prey was secured.

My fear, of course, was that he might be
mortally injured, but as it turned out he was
not. I had not the least intention of turning
him into food. My intention was to utilise

him as a messenger. I now cut off the corner of my pocket-handkerchief, the corner which bore my initials, fastened it tightly round his leg and let him go, nor did I ever see him afterwards. I was afraid that the remainder would not again use this roost, but a few nights afterwards two of them settled down here while I, as usual, lay in wait below. I struck down and secured one of them in the manner that I have already described.

To the leg of this pigeon I tied my ring. It was one which, if the bird were shot or taken, would be at once identified as mine by any member of our family, for on the inside it was engraved with a Latin inscription. It had been given to me by a great aunt a few years before. I afterwards captured a third, and to him fastened a gold shirt-stud of a peculiar pattern which I felt sure my brother Ned at least, who often examined it curiously, would at once identify as mine. After this third capture I could effect no more for a long time. The birds were quite frightened away

from that perch. Finally, not long before my
brother Edward made his way to me, I caught
a fourth. Round the leg of this messenger I
wrapped tightly a piece of my handkerchief, on
which I had inscribed with blood-characters a
statement of my whereabouts. This was the
pigeon which Harry Battersby had shot. The
characters, as the reader is aware, had been
rendered almost indistinguishable by wet. Mr.
Watkins, however, made a clever guess at the
word " window." How the constable Mulvaney
was not able to find me I shall presently explain.

CHAPTER XXIII.

A PSYCHOLOGICAL EXPERIMENT.

ONE night, about three weeks after my entomb-
ment, as I sat beside the fire thinking mourn-
fully of home and what they were all doing
there now, I thought after looking at my watch
that this was Charley's bed-hour, and the child's
singular countenance and large eyes— indeed he
seemed all eyes, like a young crow—rose before
my mind. Then I remembered having read—
I think it was in one of Bulwer Lytton's novels
—that there were some persons so finely and
sensitively organised that a person with whom
they were in close sympathy might, though
at a distance, by sustained exercise of the will
and concentration of thought, impress images
or thoughts upon their minds, the patient being
at the time in a receptive or passive mental
state. Charley, I said, is now in bed and not
yet asleep. I will at least try. I did so, and
remained for half an hour or so endeavouring

M

with the utmost concentration of thought to convey to Charley the knowledge that I was here.

For about a week I continued to do this and then gave over. I believed all the time that it was absurd, and probably only went through these mental gymnastics for want of something else to do. Once as I awoke I heard a slight thud somewhere in the long gallery, as of something falling. I did not attach any importance to it. I thought it was a stalactite falling from the roof. However, after I had breakfasted and played with my seals, I thought I would explore that gallery once more—something might have fallen or been thrown in from the outer world.

Coming to the spot where I had discovered the bones of animals, and searching round carefully in all directions, I found something at which I cried out in a passion of delight and joy. It was one of the great brown soda-cakes which were such a familiar spectacle morning and evening on the family board at home. It was grievously bruised, cracked, and gapped, but nevertheless a real *bona fide* home-made cake.

I felt at once that it was the result of my absurd experiment. Perhaps Charley had thrown in another whose fall I had not heard. I searched again, and was about to leave off when the light of my torch fell upon a large fragment of a second; the remainder no doubt was lodged above in some cleft of the winding rocky descent. The delight with which I consumed these dainties may be imagined, but infinitely greater was the joy caused by the consciousness that someone on the outside, no doubt Charley, was aware of my presence here.

In cutting that fragment of a cake to which I have already referred, my knife seemed to be resisted by something unusual. Looking for the cause I found a bit of paper which, having unfolded, I found to be a letter to me from Charley. It ran as follows :—

"My dear Jack,—I know that you are alive, and that you are in the Devil's Parlour. I send you a cake, and hope it will do you good. I saw you quite clearly, but they said I was dreaming. I will send you a cake once every second day.—Your affectionate brother,

CHARLES FREEMAN."

All doubt was now at an end; Charley knew
where I was, and though they called his vision
dreaming, I saw at once how I could communicate with the upper world and convince
folk there of my presence here. The cake had
been flung down at half-past seven in the
morning. On the second morning long before
this hour I was at the place and continued
to shout at intervals. Half-past seven passed,
eight, nine passed, but no sign came from above
and no cake. As I afterwards learned, Charley
had been sent away for change of air under
the supposition that his mind was deranged.
I seemed now as badly off as ever, and for
some time was in a frame of mind in which,
but for the seals, I might have killed myself.
The gaiety, pranks, and affection of these poor
dumb creatures prevented me from utterly losing
heart, and gradually my spirits returned, or
rather my fortitude and determination to endure
all that it might please Heaven that I should
endure rather than do a deed so cowardly and
wicked.

Like Robinson Crusoe, I remembered that though I had suffered, and might suffer a great deal, I had also a great deal to be thankful for. I might have starved miserably, whereas I was in an almost miraculous manner supplied with daily food, and instead of utter and maddening solitude I was blest with the society of these innocent, intelligent, and affectionate animals. They would now wriggle and flap themselves up the rock to my fire, and I noticed that whenever my mood was unusually low they then particularly sought to attract my attention and provoke my caresses. I called the big male Mr. Jones; his mate, of course, Mrs. Jones; and the infant Scamp. They knew their names quite well. The little one, which was, of course, the most teachable, even learned from me many tricks, which gave me, in spite of my trouble, many a hearty laugh.

About this time there was an increase in my family. One day I noticed at the entrance of the fissure which communicated with the sea a fourth pair of round, wondering eyes. It represented a strange seal which Mr. and Mrs. Jones, by various motions and frolics, seemed to be enticing into our society. Confidence is a plant of slow growth in the breast of a seal, and this seal was not drawn inwards by parental affection like Mr. and Mrs. Jones. However, not to be too tedious, I succeeded in provoking the confidence and affection of this animal also, and subsequently of others, so that before my liberation I had in all nine friends, while there were three more shy ones to whom I was making advances. I was often surrounded by the whole nine together, and likened myself to Proteus, the old man of the sea, upon whom Ulysses pounced while taking his siesta upon some Egyptian shore in the midst of his seals. When, however, too many of them came about me I used to drive some back into the water.

CHAPTER XXIV.

ATTEMPTED ESCAPE *VIÂ* THE SEALS' TUNNEL.

OF course, from the moment that I became aware of the seals' presence, the thought naturally suggested itself to me that I might be able to get out through the same tunnel or boring by which the seals came in. Immediately after securing the young seal in the manner which I have described, I took off my clothes and swam to the opening of the tunnel, which was like a small cave at the other side of the pool. Here I could only penetrate a yard or two. Dropping my feet down and feeling for the opening, I discovered it. I returned, and waiting till the water of the pool was at its lowest, swam back again, hoping that the ebb of the tide would have bared this tunnel sufficiently to enable a swimmer to get through.

I was disappointed in this. The water even

at low tide filled the tunnel and stood above
the ragged portal to the distance of between
two and three feet. By diving I might get
through, but not otherwise. This was a very
sore disappointment, for I had at first felt
joyously certain that I could swim straight
out into the open sea and so to Du-Corrig,
or better, to the shady coos where Mr. Watkins
kept his boat, and where there was a nice strand
and easy landing-place.

Amongst my many disappointments I think
there was none which affected me like that. At
one moment I saw a door of escape lying open
before me, black indeed, but comely, the
entrance, namely, of a tunnel plainly in communication with the sea; the next, in a manner
quite unexpected, I found that door barred—
barred with water. And yet I by no means
gave up all hope of eventually making my
escape by this avenue, for I was a good
swimmer and diver, though I knew well that
a man who would make his way under water
from the point where I now was to the open

sea would perhaps require three or four breaths in the course of his submarine journey. The source of this, my second spring of hope in connection with the Seals' Tunnel, will presently appear. The venture, however, upon which I had my resolution fixed I postponed executing till I should have quite tamed my seals.

First, then, I measured very carefully the distance from Curry's Window to the Seals' Pool. The cavern, it may be remembered, first trended straight inwards and then described a curve to the left, sloping downwards steadily, and at times even sharply, the whole way. This curve continuing became a recurve in the neighbourhood of the pool, so that this part of the cavern was nearer to the outer sea, by some thirty yards, than that portion of the curve which was furthest inland and away from the sea. The calculation was not easy, but here for the first and last time in my life I found my college trigonometry of some practical value to me.

My object, of course, was to discover the

distance from the mouth of the tunnel at the Seals' Pool to the other mouth by which it communicated with the sea. As the face of the sea-cliff was nearly, if not quite, vertical, my problem was not complicated by the introduction of an external element. I merely added a few yards at a guess to represent the very slight departure from perpendicularity of the face of the cliff below Curry's Window. Eventually I concluded that the tunnel, on the assumption that it would run straight, was about 170 yards long, and I still believe that this estimate was tolerably correct. For these calculations a smooth rock was my slate, and a bit of hard stone my pencil.

At this time I often thought of Sinbad the Sailor and the manner in which he escaped from *his* tomb, namely, by following the course taken by an animal along a winding passage into the open air, and of a like adventure related in Grecian history of Aristomenes the Messenian, who escaped in a similar manner, save for the fact that Aristomenes held his guiding animal, a fox, hard by the tail. But for the water I would have made my escape too as well as they, holding on to one of my seals; and Sinbad and the brave Messenian would, under my circumstances, have been quite as much at a stand as I was.

Now I knew from experience that I could dive sixty yards with ease in clear water. Consequently, diving at my full rate of speed, I would have to take breath at least thrice before reaching the sea. But then diving through a submarine tunnel, with the expectation of striking against rock with every forward drive, was obviously a very different thing from under-water swimming in the unobstructed sea. Moreover, in my transit through this tunnel I could not expect to see anything owing to the absence of light, and therefore should be obliged, as it were, to grope my way painfully along.

It might be imagined that all these considerations would at once and altogether remove from my mind the thought that I might make my escape through the Seals' Tunnel. But they did not. I argued that the fact that the tunnel was flooded at its entrance did not prove it to be flooded all the way through. Possibly, I said, the tunnel is only submarine at the two ends, and throughout its whole intervening extent I may be able to swim joyfully forward with an arched roof of rock above my head.

I knew that the outer entrance of the tunnel was submarine. I was very well acquainted with the face of the cliff outside along the sea's edge, and knew that there was no cave or fissure resembling a cave anywhere visible even at low water along this wall of cliff. Even if the tunnel throughout most of its extent were flooded, it might well be that at certain points here and there it was not flooded at all, and that I might be able from time to time to come to the surface and breathe and find myself swimming in a cave. With a few air-holes of this description I might succeed in getting through, provided they occurred at convenient intervals.

It was the 4th day of August when I first

attempted the tunnel, and when I was stronger than I had been for some time before, owing to Charley's brown bread. I took my fishing line, and fastening one end of it securely to a pointed projection of rock, wound up the rest upon a piece of timber. In the event of failure I desired to have some surer method than that of mere groping to guide me back to the place which was my home. That I might be able to determine the length of my dives, I put a row of knots upon the line with intervals of a fathom between.

I may add that before I seriously attempted the tunnel I had gradually accustomed my seals to see me without my clothes. Naturally, I feared to frighten away those creatures upon whose industry I lived. Approaching the entrance of the tunnel I dived, holding in my left hand the timber upon which the fishing line was wound, and entered the tunnel, letting the cord wind off as I went like thread from a reel. I groped along, it could hardly be called diving, with my back close to the roof of the tunnel, until, as I calculated, half my power of retaining breath was exhausted. At this point I gave over, and half swimming, half drawing myself forward by the cord which I held now in my right hand, returned as I had come.

When I rose to the surface of the pool I was aware that I could have gone some distance further without distress. Coming to land I drew in the line, and found by the knot that I had only made twelve yards. That only represented twenty-four yards to and fro, which was a considerable falling-off from the sixty yards which in unobstructed water I knew to be the length of my average submarine performances. The seals splashed about and made joyful cries on my reappearance. They were now quite accustomed to me, both on land and in the water.

I dressed, and thinking I had done enough for the first attempt, desisted from a renewal of the enterprise till next day. The next day, however, was stormy. Indeed, wild weather now supervened for more than a fortnight.

During this period I made no attempt upon the tunnel. I knew that even if I were lucky enough to get through the whole way into the ocean, I should be banged about in the surf and breakers at the foot of the cliffs, and should never be able to get home. Every day I made an observation of the weather at Curry's Window. Comparing these observations with the motions of the water in the pool, I was soon able to guess accurately the state of the weather from merely looking at the pool.

After a fortnight and two days the weather grew mild again, and having waited three days more to allow the agitation of the sea to subside, I renewed my efforts to penetrate the tunnel. I had long since eaten the last of poor Charley's cakes; my daily fare was only fish. This time I determined to proceed three yards beyond the knot. I did so, and still finding the rock above me, was about to return, when, as I was turning round and kicking, I discovered that my foot made a noise. This, of course, was a sign that I had agitated the surface of the water.

Turning again, and making a stroke forwards and upwards, I suddenly found my head in the air. My delight may be imagined. The first of the blow-holes or air-holes for which I had hoped was discovered. It might be the beginning of that arched gallery, reaching nearly to the sea, for which I had hoped. Resting for a while, I began to examine this vacant space in order to discover its nature and capabilities as well as I could in·the dark. I feared it might be so small that at full tide the water would fill it, but that was not so. I raised my voice, and the echoes clearly proved that it was of great extent. As for my hope that it might be the beginning of a long reach of tunnel, half air and half water, I was greatly disappointed to find that such was not the case. I could swim all round it. At one point the edges were so inclined that I could get clear out of the water and stand upright. As far as I could reach with my hand I could feel free space above me. This blow-hole at all events would be at my disposal whether the tide was at flood or at ebb.

It will be remembered that before starting from the Seals' Pool I had made a series of knots upon my line, each knot representing about a fathom. The distance from the entrance of the tunnel to the furthest point of this cave I found now, by means of these knots, to be twenty-eight yards. In the event of my discovering the tunnel at this point on its way to the sea, and adding. sixteen yards to the distance, viz., the space that I could traverse without being obliged to turn back, I might now consider myself as being within one hundred and thirty-six yards of the open sea, and as having virtually achieved thirty-four yards. No doubt I had a huge extent of water to get through still, but I was not daunted. On the contrary, I was filled with hope. I had found my first blow-hole, and I might find others.

"Who knows," I said, "but after passing through another submarine tunnel of half a dozen yards I might find myself in an airy gallery running almost to the edge of the

N

cliff?" I again entered the water and swam slowly all round the sides of my cave, holding on by the rock, and feeling with my feet. Eventually I thought I had found the continuation of the tunnel, and although I could not be sure, yet quite satisfied and more than satisfied with the result of this exploration, I resolved to get home now.

So I dived again, and following my clue, reappeared in the Seals' Pool, and that day dined in better spirits than I had been in at any time since my descent into this terrible cavern.

"I WAS OFTEN SURROUNDED BY THE WHOLE NINE" (*p.* 182).

CHAPTER XXV.

A DESPERATE ATTEMPT UPON THE TUNNEL.

NEXT day—for, as I think I have remarked—I observed the seasons of day and night—I made another and more determined exploration of the Seals' Tunnel. I got into my first blow-hole without difficulty, though at the cost of a bad cut on my right ankle, which pained me a good deal, and which, no doubt, bled profusely. Arrived here, I felt about for the ledge on which I had stood the day before. The tide was higher now, and the ledge covered with water, so I clambered on to it with greater ease.

I first made fast my clue and the stick on which it was wound to a projection of the rock, and afterwards, moving along the ledge, felt about in the dark with my hands. The tide was not yet at its lowest, nor would be for some time, and of course my efforts to thread the continuation of the tunnel would be best undertaken with the water at its lowest ebb, for the reasons

N 2

that I have already mentioned. In the meantime I desired to explore the cave as well as I
could. It was just possible that the continuation of the tunnel might be at this point over
land, or rather over rock. At all events, I
determined to utilise the time at my disposal
by groping about the cave. Presently I found
my right hand going round a corner of rock,
and stretching it out and away from my body,
but still in a forward direction, found nothing
there but empty space.

Scrambling into this empty space, I was
soon satisfied that I was either in the continuation of the Seals' Tunnel, or that the cave was
provided in this place with a pocket of unknown
dimensions. Though keenly bent upon exploration, I determined not to travel beyond the
sound of the water, lest I should lose my way
in the darkness. The day after I slid down
from Curry's Window I had had in the great
cavern a horrible experience of that kind, which
was a lesson to me. The sound of the water,
however, reached a great way here, owing to the

reverberation of the hollow roof. To anyone
else, no doubt, the huge sucking noises as of
some great monster drinking, and the sullen
dismal echoes of the flux and reflux of the water,
would have been very horrible and impressive.
But I was now too steeled to suffering and
horrors to take more than a utilitarian view
of those noises. I kept to that side of the
pocket by which I had first entered it, and
penetrated some twenty yards without coming to
the end or meeting with anything more note-
worthy than dry seaweed, and a good deal of
rotten drift timber.

"I know where to get fuel," I said to
myself, "should my storehouse in the big
cavern ever give out." All this time I kept
listening for the flopping sounds which my seals
would make if this were their avenue to the sea.
Hearing nothing of the kind, my hope that this
might be the tunnel subsided. Nevertheless, I
determined on some future occasion to explore
this pocket, or whatever it might be, more
thoroughly. Returning to its entrance, I slid

into the water, taking my clue with me, swam
to the point where, on the occasion of my last
visit, I seemed to have found the continuation
of the tunnel, and dived.

I went straight down, but in front of me
and on my left hand found nothing but rock;
then, turning to the right, I discovered what
seemed to be the tunnel, certainly some opening of considerable dimensions.   At this moment
something soft yet solid, and seemingly alive,
pushed against my breast and throat.   I was so
frightened that in my terror I dropped the clue
and sucked in a quantity of water.   Recovering
my self-control I got to the surface as quickly
as I could.   Fortunately I was only at the
mouth of the tunnel.   Had I been in the interior   when   this   happened I   should almost
certainly have been drowned, so frightened was
I by this mysterious collision.   Hardly had I
gained the surface when I guessed the cause of
my alarm.   It was certainly one of my seals.
Presently I heard the well-known cry, and the
poor beast pressed up against me in the dark.

It was a female seal who was very much attached to me. I used to call her the Plaintiff.

Though my terror was allayed, I felt myself unequal to the task of any further exploration of the tunnel just then. Accordingly, feeling my way round the cave till I came to the ledge which was near the entrance of the first portion of the tunnel, I dived and got home without further accident, and succeeded in drawing back my clue, which I feared might have stuck fast somewhere.

Here I may add that owing, I suppose, to the original heat of my temperament, or perhaps the possession of a fair share of fat, for I might be described as stout rather than thin, I could remain in water longer than any other swimmer of my acquaintance. On the present occasion I was dispirited and out of sorts, but not cold. Yet, having dined, I felt brisk and vigorous again. This day I dined on steaks of turbot— I mention it because it was the only flat-fish that my seals brought me during the whole term of my imprisonment.

It now occurred to me that if I could make a fire in that cave off the first blow-hole, it would be of great service to me in my next attempt to traverse the continuation of the tunnel there. But how to bring fire thither was certainly a difficulty. I could not bring a burning brand with me, swimming under water a distance of sixteen yards. That was plain. I now re-examined that pocket of my coat in which I had found the loose powder originally, though I knew that there could be little or none left. After making that piece of tinder or touch-cloth by which I kindled my first fire, I had turned the pocket inside out that the loose grains might fall upon it and so help towards the ignition. On examining this pocket now by the light of my fire I noticed that the bottom of it was quite black. I guessed the cause at once. Some time last winter my jacket had got thoroughly soaked with rain, and the bottom of the pocket was steeped in solution of gunpowder.

I touched the black lining with the tip of my tongue and recognised the acrid taste. I now saw my way clearly towards the making of a second fire. I cut out the black part of the lining and bestowed it in my purse. It was the first leathern purse I ever owned, bought since I went to college, for my school-boy purse was a netted one with steel rings and little bunch of steel pendants at each end. My father, I remember, never gave in to the leathern clasp purse; he used a netted one with rings as long as he lived. Then I took a piece of my line, and having doubled the purse, bound it round strongly with the cord and made it perfectly water-tight.

Next day, some two hours before low water, I stripped, took my knife and the rolled-up purse in my teeth, the clue also as usual in my hand, and dived through the tunnel, came up in the blow-hole, and clambered into the dry part of the cavern. I placed the purse and knife in a spot where I could easily find them again, and having first dried my hands in the crisp sea-weed which was abundant here, proceeded to select the brittlest and most crumbling timber. Such was embedded everywhere in the seaweed. Then I kept moving about, striking sparks from the rocks with my knife till I found a projection which seemed to emit them in a more brilliant manner than the rest. Now I soon learned what an assistance to me in my former attempt of this kind was the loose powder which I was then in a position to sprinkle upon the touch-cloth. Though the sparks were sometimes so bright as to reveal clearly not only the touch-cloth but my whole hand, and though they seemed to fly right into the cloth, they produced no other result than these fleeting illuminations.

I believe I was nearly an hour at this exercise, and at last gave over, my wrist being thoroughly tired.

As I now sat reflecting it occurred to me that the cloth would have a better chance of catching fire if I presented its edges to the sparks, and also if I were to fray those edges into fluff. " Better still," I thought, " fray a good deal of those edges into fluff. It will then

be sheer tow, which, saturated as it is in solution of gunpowder, *must* catch fire."

I did this. Then I struck the rock again
with my knife, and at the first spark that went
rightly into the tow the latter caught fire, spluttering and fizzing up gloriously. I had my
little heap of crumbled touch-wood ready at
hand all this time. In short, after a very few
minutes I stood beside a large and brightly
burning fire. There was plenty of timber at
hand for the feeding of it. The whole cave was
brilliantly lighted up—roof, sides, and the level
floor of dark but gleaming water. So much of
the cave as was just above the water was nearly
quite round, and presented the appearance of an
inverted bowl. After a short observation of the
blow-hole I turned my attention to the pocket.
The entrance was not wide, but the cave within
expanded into great dimensions. As I knew,
however, that this pocket, huge pouch, or whatever it might be termed, was no better for me
than a blind alley leading no whither, I postponed its exploration. I was not here to make

discoveries, but to make my way out, if by God's grace, and my own swimming and diving, it might in any way be effected.

It was now low water, as I judged by the appearance of the ledge. Then, unfastening my clue, and commending myself to the protection of the Almighty, I swam across the pool to the place where I knew was the sea-going entrance of the tunnel, and dived. As I had knots all along the line marking the yards, I knew exactly the rate of my progress. I had not gone ten yards when, feeling nothing above me with my right hand, I slowly rose, and presently found my head above water.

This was an unexpected good fortune. I had found my second blow-hole. I was certainly ten yards nearer to the sea, and how many more besides would depend on the size of this second cavern. I swam round its edges and found that it was of exceeding small dimensions, only about three yards in diameter, in fact quite literally a blow-hole and nothing else.

It had this advantage, however, viz., that the entrance of the continuation of the tunnel was apparent or, more correctly, palpable. I felt the edges of the tunnel quite distinctly with my feet, and the movement of the water there, for the tide had turned. Again I dived and continued groping forward to a distance of fourteen yards, but still felt the rock above me. Most reluctantly I turned back at this point, for I knew that a good half of my power of retaining breath was exhausted. My return journey, however, was the easier, for I assisted myself by drawing in the line, which was excellent strong whip-cord. Yet, even so, I was almost at the furthest limit of my powers when I reached the small blow-hole. There I remained for a few minutes blowing and panting. My return thence to the cup-shaped cave where my fire burned was easy. Moreover I could see before me the reflection of the light in the water, which had upon my mind the effect of a friendly beckoning and welcoming hand.

Clambering up to my fire, I sat down beside

it brooding and pondering. It was now quite plain to me that escape by the Seals' Tunnel was only possible on one condition, viz., that I should stake my life on the chance—the chances being enormously against success. I knew that in my dive from the second blow-hole towards the sea I had done my very best, gone forward to the last yard, exhausting the full half of all my power of holding my breath. True, there might have been a breathing-place one yard beyond the point at which I had turned back ; but then, again, there might not be any such blow-hole at all between the second of my breathing-places and the sea, and from that point to the sea, on the assumption that the tunnel ran quite straight, there was a distance of more than one hundred yards according to the most favourable computation. Were I to dive again from the second blow-hole with no intention of returning, only with the intention of pushing forward till I should be drowned or find another breathing-spot, I might make twenty-four yards, or even by desperate determination and such power as God might graciously give me, make even thirty yards. There, then, if I met with no breathing-place, I should be miserably smothered and drowned.

I knew that if I were to make this desperate stroke for freedom, the sooner I delivered it the better, for my physical strength, owing to a diet of fish repeated day after day, was failing. In mind I was still vigorous, but physically I was decidedly weaker than when I entered the cavern. A few days before this, I endeavoured to move a pebble which the day after my imprisonment I had been able to raise a little, though not so far as to turn it right over. On this second occasion I could only just stir it in its place. After a while I got up and explored the cavern, lighting new fires at convenient intervals. It was indeed a great and august chamber of rock, fit to be the temple of some gloomy superstition, but I discovered there nothing of any importance, not even sound timber. This pocket, like the great cavern, had not been visited by the sea for many years.

The drift timber there, though abundant enough, crumbled as I handled it.

I covered up the embers of the fire near the blow-hole with ashes to keep it alive, and returned through the tunnel to my own cave. That evening I brooded long and earnestly over the dreadful problem. The making of steps along the slope up to Curry's Window would be the work of many months, perhaps of years. If I adopted that other desperate alternative, viz., a despairing, headlong and rushing dive through the tunnel, I should either escape at once or at once die, and so be released from all my troubles. Then it seemed to me that to take such a step, with all the chances so greatly against success, was like suicide—a crime which I had been brought up to regard as perhaps the most heinous and awful of all crimes.

When I awoke in the morning it seemed to me as if I had somehow made up my mind and come to a determination while I slept. At the time I regarded this as a divine illumination vouchsafed to my prayers for guidance and light.

Possibly enough, for the human mind is very deceitful, I finally decided against the bolder and more daring course sheerly from want of courage to put it into execution; and, truly, the thought of being smothered with salt water in the submarine darkness of the tunnel would have been enough to appal and unman a bolder spirit than mine.

Yet, indeed, I do not believe that I was turned aside by fear from the adoption of the more daring and perilous course. I have to observe, however, that from this day forward a certain lassitude, inertness, and lack of spirit grew upon me, mainly caused by my low diet, but noticeably beginning to appear on this particular day, owing to the complete and final frustration of all the high and joyful hopes which I had so long entertained in connection with the Seals' Tunnel. There, within a few yards of me, lay the gate and entrance of a road leading to light, liberty, home, and happiness; yet I could not traverse it, so charged was it all with salt water. My poor seals went

o

there freely out and in half a dozen times in a
day, but I could not, though indeed I tried and
did my best.

While Charley's brown bread came down to
me I was strong. When that failed, and I had
nothing but fish to eat, I slowly day by day
grew weak. I did not feel despondency so
much as a certain lassitude and a tendency to
do nothing but ruminate and half sleep, so that
sometimes even the task of feeding my fire
seemed to require a great effort of will before it
could be effected.

CHAPTER XXVI.

AT CURRY'S WINDOW.

THIS lassitude, however, came over me slowly, and at first imperceptibly. When I made up my mind not to attempt to rush the tunnel, I was vigorous enough. Accordingly I at once commenced a labour which I had always intended, but had put off till it became certain that I had no other way of escape. As the reader may remember, I made no very serious effort in any direction until I had first established such relations with my dumb companions as would ensure me a supply of food, for I perceived that no mode of possible escape offered itself which did not involve time and labour, and that the food problem was the first to which I should devote myself.

At half-past nine o'clock, on the morning of the 9th of September, I began to cut steps in the incline leading up to Curry's Window. Not

o 2

long after my imprisonment, I had scored the
rock here with my knife. It was limestone, of
the hardest and closest grain imaginable. For
cutting steps I used the brass reel of my fishing-
rod, which, fortunately, had been caught in the
interstice between two great boulders. I broke
it into pieces, and used piece after piece till the
bit used as chisel was worn too small. The
little worn-out fragments I put carefully by,
intending to melt them, if I could, and fuse
them into one piece afterwards when the
usable pieces should be exhausted. My precious
knife I resolved not to use up till the last extremity, for I could not tell in what way it
might yet be necessary to me.

I worked steadily at these steps, using first
the right hand and then the left. With plenty
of time and plenty of brass I could certainly
make my way out of the den, but I perceived
after I had finished the first step, which was in
fact only a little crevice into which I could
insert my bare toes, that my supply of metal
would be worn out long before the necessary

niches or footholds could be made. I worked standing on the top of the rude bone and timber ladder, whose construction I have already described, and this ladder rested upon the heap of stones, gravel, bones, and sea-weed. The sea-weed was, in fact, my bed and bed-clothes. Every morning I brought it hither, and at night carried it back to the Seal Pond, which was my head-quarters.

It will be seen that by utilising the sea-weed in this manner I saved the making of a step or two, which, of course, meant a great deal to me. Though my supply of brass wore out fast, my strength seemed to wear out faster. I became very weak—so much so, that the cutting of the second step took five days longer than that of the first; and that of the third took three whole weeks, and I was conscious that my strength was still fading away. That this arose from an exclusively fish diet, helped a little, I confess, with edible sea-weeds gathered in the Seals' Pool, I had a rather curious proof. My marine retainers brought me so much food that

it was an embarrassment to me. What I did
not want I used to fling towards the mouth of
the tunnel at the ebb of the tide. The tunnel
was thus a sort of refuse pipe. One day I took
a large haddock, to which I fastened a stone,
and flung it into the pool, where, of course, it
sank to the bottom. I went to my graving
work as usual, and when I returned and held
my torch over the spot where I had thrown the
fish, saw a fine lobster, half-covering the white
haddock—evidently feasting upon it.

I thrust the butt end of my rod to him,
which he at once seized upon viciously with one
of his claws, so that I drew him safely to land.
I made my supper upon him, relishing well the
change of diet, and did not leave a small claw
unbroken or its contents not eaten. Next day
I worked—or thought I worked—better. I did
afterwards occasionally catch a lobster or crab in
this manner, and noticed the same result. Still
I was very weak, and more than once spent a
whole day in perfect idleness beside my fire—
such was my lassitude and extreme exhaustion.

Also I grew very drowsy. I was never more than half asleep, and not often wide awake. My seals, sporting in the pool or gathering round me barking and whimpering as I lay, the vast surrounding darkness, the noises and echoes, the craggy and illuminated corners of rock above, began to look very dreamlike. I was often asleep, or more asleep than awake, while I kept feebly scoring the incline at the window. Finally, this apathy or weakness, or both, grew so upon me, that I almost ceased to have even the desire of escaping, and longed inexpressibly to fall fast asleep and forget everything; which, nevertheless, I was unable to do.

I was at this time never rightly awake, and never rightly asleep. When I first became seriously conscious of my failing strength, and knew or guessed the cause, I thought of killing a seal, not one of my pets and friends, but the next strange seal which might show itself. But when the next appeared I was too inert to set about the undertaking, nor indeed did I know how to set about it, for the creature was very shy.

Curiously enough, though I now ate very little, I did not feel hunger. In fact, I was dying by inches; all my vital powers, bodily and mental, seemed to be slowly and painlessly fading away. This lethargic habit began to oppress me seriously in the beginning of October, and continued into November.

CHAPTER XXVII.

THE GHOST.

ONCE while I was in this lax and spiritless condition, highly nervous, too, as I have no doubt,
I became suddenly aware that something was
passing me by, not in front, but behind me, and
very close. Of course I saw nothing. The
sensation was something like that of a person
who, in a dark room, becomes aware, he does
not know how, of the presence and proximity
of another person. My fire was on the top of
a smooth inclined rock, or rather on the smooth
inclined floor of the cavern, which, from where
I lay, sloped rather sharply down to the Seals'
Pool.

My hearth, so to speak, and the floor immediately around it, was level. I pitched upon
this spot as my resting-place because from it the
light of the fire not only illuminated the pool
and allowed me to see my seals at their gambols

there, but threw certain pleasant reflections on the rugged projections of the opposite wall of the cave, viz., that on the same side with the pool. Between the fire and the other wall of the cavern at this point there was only the distance of four or five feet.

I usually lay or sat facing the pool, therefore, with my back to this wall. It was between me and it, and close behind me, that the thing, whatever it was, seemed to pass. I was not at all afraid of ghosts, though, indeed, once before, when a school-boy, I had a very singular experience not so unlike that which I am now about to relate. Nevertheless, as I have mentioned, I was not at all afraid of ghosts. More than once, when I wanted timber for any work I might have had on hand, I had sallied forth at night to get what I required in an adjoining graveyard. I had never even taken an imaginative delight in ghost stories, which seemed to give other boys such singular and unaccountable pleasure. I fancy I was of too active a habit of mind and body for that form of pleasure. At the moment I was thinking of home, and even of a home scene more calculated than others to dispel evil imaginations. I was thinking, in fact, of our household—the family, the domestics, and two outdoor servants—assembled in the breakfast room at family prayers, and of my father's appearance and manner when—as was his custom—he prayed *extempore*, including in his petitions many things of local and family interest. Like nearly all the rural Irish clergy of that time, his principles and practices were of the Low Church or Evangelical school.

While so brooding, reflecting, and imagining, as I sat over my fire—sleepy, too, as I usually was in those days—suddenly I felt a curious sensation of cold, and then became aware of this thing, person, or whatever it was, passing me by. I dare say my hair stood on end. I certainly felt the most extraordinary sensation, as of a thousand needles driven into my head, and such a sense of horror and fear as I never experienced before, and hope I never shall again. I am ashamed to say, too, that I

screamed—and with what a noise that scream
rang through the long and lofty cavern, with its
various galleries, can be imagined. I heard a
great plashing in the Seals' Pool. It was my
seals plunging into the water when they heard
the scream. I ran down to the water, quaking
in every limb—or, rather, I tumbled forward in
that direction, for I remember falling more than
once, and afterwards found my knees badly cut,
as well as the lower part of the palms of my
hands near the wrists. In fact, I fled to my
seals for protection against this thing. They
were alive, and real, and natural, and I hastened
to them quite instinctively, as one might to any
human companionship from the dread of that
which was uncanny, horrible, and supernatural.
But I had effectually frightened the seals. They
had plunged through the water into their tunnel,
and disappeared.

Presently, however, I saw them again in the
opening of the tunnel—four or five black heads
close together, with their round eyes, filled with
wonder, glittering in the light shed upon them

from my fire, which was blazing brightly at the same time. A little before I was alarmed in that manner I had heaped up some fresh timber, which was now sending out a good blaze. I spoke to my seals, called them to me, and in a short time they came. The moment I laid my hands on their heads I felt calmed, and although I still quaked, I was aware that my courage and self-control were returning. I knew I had need of them, for I was certain that this thing would come again.

The apparition, as I was aware, had passed me from the right hand to the left as I sat; that is to say, coming from the interior of the cave and going towards the entrance, or, in other words, from the gallery in which was the tomb and going towards Curry's Window. "It will pass this way again returning," I said to myself. I am not sure that I am speaking correctly when I say that I determined to watch for its reappearance. It would be perhaps more true to say that my gaze was drawn in the direction of the fire by a horrible fascination. After a time

which seemed an age, but which was exactly five
minutes and twenty-seven seconds (how I am so
exact as to the length of the interval I shall
afterwards explain), the thing reappeared,
passing, as before, between the fire and the
wall of the cavern.

As on the former occasion, I felt first a
curious and uncanny sensation of cold; then a
quite formless dark shape (if a thing formless
may be described as a shape), surrounded by a
mist-like pale smoke, passed between the fire
and the rock, moving now from the right to the
left—that is, from my right hand to my left—as
I sat amongst the seals, and disappearing in the
obscurity that filled the interior parts of the
cavern. Its movement was perfectly even and
regular—a steady, gliding progression. This
time I did not scream, though I shook and
trembled violently. Now, at least, I was
thoroughly awake and alert, with all my
faculties quite preternaturally active.

The listless, semi-comatose condition in
which I had been sunk for so many days

disappeared. It came on again later on, however, as I shall presently describe. Between six and seven minutes afterwards the thing passed again, and so continued to pass for some hours, always seeming to take a longer time to do the distance from the fire into the interior and back again than that which lay between the fire and the entrance of the cavern. The apparition continued to present generally the same appearance, save that the darkness which was in the midst of the luminous haze seemed to be more distinct. Sometimes I thought it presented the outlines of a man, and once I imagined that I made out clearly the head and shoulders. I noticed, also, after the lapse of about two hours, that the central darkness was not quite dark; and I distinguished there some faint indications of colour.

I was now so far recovered from the state of abject terror into which I had been thrown by the apparition, that I determined to snatch a burning faggot from the fire and kindle for myself a new fire in the neighbourhood of my seals. I saw that if I did not do so my fire would presently burn out, and that I would not be able to kindle another.

Inspired with a desperate courage by this horrible thought (the thought, namely, that I might henceforward be compelled to live not only in cold, but in darkness, and also with this thing in the darkness), I determined, come what might of it, to save my fire. Accordingly, waiting till the apparition had passed on its way into the interior of the cavern, I hastened forward, and returned with a burning ember. I had previously brought some timber from that pocket filled with drift-wood. I endeavoured to kindle a fire with the aid of the ember. This attempt failed, and seeing the fire now very low, regardless of all consequences, I rushed forward again and returned with three or four small embers, holding the still unignited ends of these in my hands, and keeping their red points together. This time I succeeded, and in spite of the presence of the apparition, felt a singular sense of joy and satisfaction as my driftwood caught fire and sent up a bright blaze.

I was still desperately frightened. While manipulating my firewood, the sticks frequently fell from my hands, which shook as if I were suffering from ague. Yet, frightened as I was, I determined to do battle even with *it* for my fire. To be alone in the darkness, alone but with the apparition, seemed more frightful than anything that might befall me in keeping my fire alive. Truly I was at death's door, but I was determined to die at least "in the light," and see this thing, rather than in the darkness and altogether at its mercy. I now looked steadily at the place where it had been moving to and fro, but though I looked a long time I saw nothing. Then I began to think, not that the manifestation had been an evil dream, but that it was an ocular delusion, an affection of the optic nerve, an imagination resulting from the low fever that preyed upon me, accompanied by that unusual lethargy and sense of physical and mental depression.

CHAPTER XXVIII.

THE GHOST TAKES AN UNEXPECTED SHAPE.

I DID not see the apparition for some days after that, and began to entertain the hope that it would not again come to plague me; but at midnight of the fourth day it appeared again, and this time not as an unshaped blot of darkness surrounded by mist, but exhibiting a very distinct shape—the shape of a man. As on the first occasion, a sudden premonitory chill, like the passing of an ice-cold wind, struck cold and terror alike into the very marrow of my bones. I knew now what was coming. Will it this time, I thought, pass by me, or interfere with me in my new place, or keep to its old beat?

I kept my eyes fixed upon the wall of rock where my old fireplace had been, and which was faintly lit by the illumination of my new fire. Then, presently, I saw the figure of a tall man striding noiselessly along, proceeding just as that shapeless blot had done from the interior of the cavern, and moving towards the entrance. The outline of his form was perfectly distinct, the colours and the lines within the form were blurred and dim. So far as I could judge, in the nervous condition into which I was thrown by the reappearance of the phantom, the figure wore a mantle and a kilt reaching to the knees, the legs being otherwise bare. In a horrible condition of alarm, but still exercising over myself a certain self-control, I awaited its return. After what seemed to be the usual lapse of time, it re-passed along the illuminated wall of rock, and as silently as before.

On this occasion either the outlines and colours were more clear and visual, or the fact that I was not now taken by surprise enabled me to observe the phenomenon with less agitation and alarm. This man—if man it was— wore his hair long, wore also a beard. His mantle was red, and on his breast I saw something glittering. It was plainly a man—a man,

p 2

dead or alive—but the figure was still very dim and blurred.

In this manner it continued to pass and re-pass, while I remained as if glued to the spot on which I sat. Though the fire was burning now very low, I either forgot to feed it, or did not dare to do so owing to my agitation or the fear of attracting the phantom in my direction— I forget now which. So low did the fire fall that at length I with difficulty could distinguish the moving shape as it passed and re-passed. Then one of my seals came up to me and uttered its cheerfullest and friendliest cries.

The noise made by this poor animal, utterly unconscious, apparently, of any dread presence in the cavern, recalled me to myself. I laid a little fresh drift-wood on the fire, and when the blaze shot up saw clearly once more the apparition moving from the entrance towards the interior— viz., from my right hand to my left. I waited for its return, but it did not return. I looked at my watch; it was a little after a quarter to three a.m. When the ghost had commenced to walk

I did not know, save that it was somewhere about midnight. I remained awake for hours after this, and at last fell into a broken slumber haunted by disagreeable images, so that I was pleased to be again awake. Next night, when the hands of my watch approached the midnight hour, I sat up, observant, though alarmed and trembling.

Of course, I apprehended that this dread elder tenant of the cavern, in spite of his past harmless behaviour, would at some time challenge my right to be there, or in one way or another attack me. Now, though I don't wish to boast of my courage—and, indeed, I believe it is no proof of a chicken-heart to be afraid of a ghost—yet having had many hours to reflect over this singular phenomenon, I was determined, come what might, to resist it in that event; at least not to permit this man, for, indeed, a man he seemed, to frighten me out of my senses, and then destroy me at his leisure. I knew that ghosts, if any such existed, were unsubstantial, not to be injured by weapons, and presenting no purchase even to the bravest hands, yet it never occurred to me that this ghost could have been of that unsubstantial nature. Though he made no sound whatsoever, beyond what I presently recognised to be the mere figment of my imagination, creating for the phantom a footfall whenever its foot seemed to touch the hard ground, yet otherwise it seemed perfectly substantial, a solid mass of apparently human flesh.

It quite concealed the face of the rock as it passed by, obliterating in its passage the illuminated points and projections there, which instantly shone out again after it had gone by. More than that, I remembered having distinctly seen its shadow. I don't say that these reasonings passed through my mind then, and I only refer to them now to justify the conviction which I entertained, that this being was not a ghost in the ordinary sense of the word, but a substantial thing that might lay hold on me, and drag me by the hair through the cavern, perhaps to its den. I never doubted that it was a thing which could lay hold on me, and also upon which

I might lay hold, and with which I might struggle, and which possibly, God helping me, I might overcome. Indeed, I did not forget my prayers, while firmly resolving in my own mind not to be destroyed without a struggle.

I prayed incessantly, and though I felt greater calm, self-control, and even strength, as the result of my prayers, did not observe that the use of the sacred names exercised the least influence on the apparition. It is true, indeed, that my murmuring of those holy names was quite inaudible. I felt that to stand up and, in the name of Jesus Christ, bid the spectre go, would be an act of war, so to speak, and that as long as it should leave me alone and not come nearer, it would be more prudent not to proceed to such extremities. This was, no doubt, weak, but allowances must be made for my very helpless condition, immured here, far from men, in this tomb, with a fellow-tenant of that horrible character. So far the ghost had not interfered with me. On this the third appearance of the spectre, its shape, outline, and the interior lines and colours were completely and distinctly visible. I saw now pass before me, with a long, steady, and even stride, not indeed the tallest man I have ever seen, but amongst the tallest. I have never seen, nor ever cared to see, one of those unfortunate human beings who are hawked about the world as a spectacle and a show on account of their prodigious size.

The man who now, almost exactly at twelve o'clock, began to pass and re-pass a few yards away from me, was as tall as one of the taller of the Dublin policemen, of a bulk, too, and length of limb corresponding with his height, and, indeed, very finely formed. The something which I had formerly noticed as glittering upon his breast, I now saw to be a round wheel, seemingly of gold; but why the man wore a wheel on his breast I could not at first understand. After he had passed and re-passed a few times I discovered that this was the ring of an enormous brooch.

I could see the two ends of the pin of this brooch, one knobbed on the man's right

shoulder, and the other pointed, on his left.
The figure was that of an antique warrior, but
not at all of the conventional type with which
one is familiar.   He wore a tall brazen helmet.
His hair, yellowish, or rather sandy, neither
lustrous nor curling, fell on his shoulders.   His
beard and moustache were not exactly red, but
more inclined to red than the hair of his head.
His mantle was a dark crimson, with loose
thrums apparently of gold thread, or thread
stained to that resemblance, glittering along the
borders.   What I had at first imagined to be a
kilt, I now saw was only the lower part of a
shirt or loose tunic, gathered at the waist by a
dark-red belt, and falling thence in loose folds to
the knees.   It was striped vertically white and
red.   He wore shoes of a brown or dun colour,
but furnished with clasps or latchets of some
description of metal unknown, which I could
perceive shining.   He wore tight-fitting hose
of a dun colour, which were not laced or
gartered anywhere.

When he went towards the interior from the

entrance of the cave I could see distinctly a short
sword, which hung down quite vertically on his
left thigh. The scabbard seemed to be made of
some reddish kind of wood. It was fastened
with bright-headed rivets, and was shod at either
end with a substance which looked like gold—
but was brighter. The handle of the sword
looked like ivory, but was rather duller in hue
than ivory should be. Otherwise he was unarmed.
In fact, generally, he presented the appearance
of a warrior of ancient times. His right arm
always hung down by his side, the left hand was
passed under the mantle and lay on his breast,
taking hold upon something there—I fancy
upon the strap of his sword—what antiquarians, I
think, call a baldrick. His head was bent a little
forwards, and his shoulders were slightly rounded
—at all events, his gait was not quite erect.
His attitude was that of a man pondering profoundly upon some intricate problem, and pacing
to and fro quite immersed in calculations and
ruminations concerning its solution. Though I
watched him pass and re-pass at least a hundred

times, his carriage and mode of holding his hands
never varied in the least from what I have described. His bearing, I say, was that of a man
deeply reflecting, but there was no sign or token
of reflection whatsoever in his face. There was
truly no speculation in those eyes. Otherwise
his face suggested life rather than death, for it
was of a good colour, somewhat ruddy in the
cheeks, and well bronzed otherwise. The eyes
alone, so wide open, staring, and lustreless,
suggested death.

As to his age, he seemed to be about forty.
I may add, at the risk of being too minute, that
on his brooch were five good-sized eyes of glass
—or some substance duller than glass—and that
on his left temple there was a scar running from
the roots of his hair to the outer extremity of
the corresponding eyebrow. I had plenty of
time and opportunity to make these observations,
for after his second appearance the ghost continued to walk every night exactly at twelve
o'clock, and ceased to walk at about three.
Invariably, also, his walking terminated in the

interior portion of the cave, and in that gallery
at the end of which was the strange tomb which
I have described.   After passing me on the way
to Curry's Window he did not re-pass for five
minutes and twenty-seven seconds.   The passage
into the interior and back occupied almost exactly
six minutes.

Although the reader will, of course, attribute
this apparition wholly to the diseased state of
my nerves and imagination, and although such
is my own belief too, in a sense, yet it is singular that the apparition, supposing it to be
such, should have assumed exactly this form
and garb.   I never saw a man dressed in that
style.   I had never even seen a picture of a man
so dressed; for, although the flowing mantle, long
hair, straight-hanging sword, and kilt, form the
usual get-up of antique warriors on the stage and
in pictures, the big brooch was quite strange and
novel, even to my imagination.

Such antique warriors, too, in pictures or on
the stage, appear gartered to the knee, and
always carry a shield on their arm or strapped to

their backs. This figure had no shield, wore hose, not stockings, and was not gartered. Consequently, if the apparition sprang from my imagination, and from the imagination projected itself into visuality in this remarkable manner, my imagination was able to produce something that my eyes had never seen, either in the world of reality or in the world of art, and something that the imagination had never at any time consciously conceived at all. Another singular circumstance is this: I knew that this cave was the cave of Curry the smuggler. I had already associated the idea of the tomb which I had discovered with him. Now, my notion of a smuggler was that which is commonly entertained by all boys and young men, viz., a stout, strong, burly man of a sea-faring type, wearing top-boots, and pistols stuck in his belt. Having had plenty of time for reflection, the thought of Curry the smuggler, in this highly conventional form, *i.e.*, the melodramatic smuggler, had been frequent in my mind; and since I discovered the tomb, the notion that Curry's ghost might haunt the cavern had very frequently arisen in my numerous broodings and cogitations. I did not, indeed, seriously entertain the thought of Curry's ghost inhabiting the cave, but the fancy or idea, as ideas will, had oftentimes passed idly through my mind. Yet the apparition, when it did come, was as unlike a smuggler as it was unlike a nineteenth-century man of fashion. I, too, am now convinced—indeed, I did not leave that cave without the conviction that this spectre was the creature of my imagination, wrought up by low diet and solitude to a preternatural degree of potency and activity.

But of this, too, I am convinced—that the imagination in some persons, and under abnormal circumstances, has a power which few people suspect, and unconsciously to ourselves, is fed and sustained by a kind of knowledge and by forms of experience which never came within the range of the imagining person. Before concluding, I shall relate something which seems to provide some faint clue to my very remarkable preternatural experiences in Curry's Cave.

After the spectre's second appearance it continued to walk for five nights, beginning and ending its mysterious beat or promenade at exactly the same time each night, and taking exactly the same course on each occasion. By degrees I began to be so accustomed to its presence that I sometimes even broiled and ate my fish while the ghost went to and fro, and once I lessened, by nearly half, the distance which separated us, in order to observe him and his habiliments more closely and accurately. On this occasion its eyes seemed, on a nearer view, to present so terrible an expression, that the moment it passed I withdrew swiftly to the proximity of my fire and seals, and did not again venture one yard away from the opposite wall of the cave.

The excitement caused by the apparition had roused me, to a considerable degree, from the lethargy into which I had been before fast sinking, and, indeed, had sunk almost past recall. Indeed, but for the ghost I think I should have died in that cave, so stupid, sleepy, and

indifferent to all things was I fast growing.
The ghost, at least, had the merit of keeping me
rather broad awake for some days, and all my
faculties on the alert. Otherwise I might have
succumbed before the arrival of the relief which
was now about to make such a difference, both
in my condition of mind and body and in my
prospects. The excitement had this almost
immediate good effect, that when the first in-
tensity of it had passed away I ate rather more
broiled fish than I had done for many days before
the coming of the apparition. So, when the
relief did arrive, I was in a condition to utilise it.

"I FOUND A FAT SHEEP LYING MOTIONLESS ON THE GROUND" (*p.* 241).

CHAPTER XXIX.

ALL ABOUT MUTTON.

On the 12th day of that month my lethargy was dissipated, and at the same time the ghost laid in a singular manner. As I sat beside my fire nodding, as my custom was, I was startled into sudden animation by a loud yet dull thud, as of some heavy body falling in the long gallery. Snatching a brand from the fire, I hastened thither, and at the spot where the bones formerly lay, and where I had discovered the brown cakes, found a fat sheep lying motionless on the ground.

I was now wide awake and active, and even excited. When I heard the noise I guessed at once what caused it. The ghost was no impediment to me, for it was only about two o'clock in the afternoon, and his solemn marchings to and fro would not commence till midnight. The

Q

sheep was quite dead. I bled her as she lay,
and though practically ignorant of the butcher's
art, skinned her partially, cut out certain layers
from the breast, and returning to my fire, roasted
them. I was not consciously hungry, and had
no longing for flesh-food, but being now wide
awake and actively intelligent, I knew that
meat would do me good, and that if I was not
to die I should eat it.

The odour and smell of the frizzling chops,
however, at once awakened a furious appetite.
I ate with a relish, and returning to the carcase
of the unfortunate sheep, hacked off two more
chops, broiled, and ate them. I would have
eaten more, but I knew how dangerous such
indulgence would be after long abstinence.
Then I drank copiously from that little glittering pencil of descending water to which I have
referred. I used to drink of it sometimes by
the simple process of opening my mouth to
receive it—at least, when I was in good health
and spirits. Finally, I filled myself a pipe
of tobacco, and enjoyed a good smoke, a luxury

in which I had not indulged for a long time. In fact, I had quite lost my taste for it.

Finding myself unusually gay and vigorous, I might almost say defiant and pugnacious, I determined this night to accost the apparition, and that, too, not in the gentlest manner. I did not then suspect that my weak and nervous condition had anything to do with the presence of the apparition. Twelve o'clock passed, and one—yet I saw absolutely nothing that night, nor did I ever afterwards once perceive either that antique martial figure or anything at all suggestive of the uncanny and supernatural as long as I remained in the cave. I have heard and read of various methods of laying ghosts and exorcising evil spirits. Mutton chops, nicely broiled, and eaten by an extremely hungry lad, laid my ghost, and laid him effectually. . Divine Providence saved me my life and my reason on this occasion.

I don't think I am a boaster, but from what I recollect I am convinced that if the ghost had appeared that night, as he had been in the habit

Q 2

of appearing for so many nights previously, I should not only have challenged him, but, if unanswered, would have barred his path. Familiarity breeds contempt. Every night, for more than three hours on each occasion, I had been now for weeks watching the sturdy passage of this sinister figure, as it paced to and fro along the north wall of the cavern.

I slept soundly that night, and awoke in the morning alert, energetic, and ravenous. Of course I attacked the sheep again, but what was my surprise to find on this occasion another great brown cake close beside the sheep, quite fresh, and seemingly baked on the previous day. Moving around with my torch, I discovered some half-dozen others, some of them quite stale. It was evident that Charley had again been at work, and seemingly was now enabled, without let or hindrance, to roll me down a cake every second day, as he had promised.

Having now both mutton and bread to eat with it, I rapidly recovered my health and strength, and the knowledge that one at least of my brothers was firmly convinced that I was at the bottom of the Devil's Parlour filled me again with hope. I skinned and jointed my sheep, and collecting from various little hollows near the pool all the salt procurable, proceeded to corn as much of it as it was not likely that I should eat fresh, rubbing the salt well in with my hands. As my supply of salt was limited, I eked it out by soaking each piece of mutton in the tidal water. After each steeping I dried the piece at the fire and again plunged it in the salt water, and between times I rubbed the salt vigorously into it. Indeed, I succeeded in preserving the whole sheep very well. With renewed energy and zeal I now returned to my suspended labours at the window, and worked there with a will, and from early morning till late at night with little intermission. My bread came to me as regularly as it did to the prophet at the brook Cherith. I had bread, meat and fish, and even vegetables—if one can count edible sea-weed as such. All was going well with me.

Early in December my last piece of brass had worn too small to be of service. I melted all the little pieces which I had saved, made for myself thereby a very bright brand-new chisel, and scored away industriously. Though I knew that this tool would not bring me to the sill— that it would be worn out before I could effect my deliverance—yet not once did my heart and hope flag. I had brass buttons on my clothes; I had my watch, watch-guard, and chain—I would melt them too into a chisel. Even with flint stones, when all the metal gave out, I could do something. I now began to feel confident that if only my life were spared long enough I would carve my way out of my den. This energy and vigour seemed to be all my own, generated in my unconquerable will, and yet it all came from that poor " clifted " sheep and my brother Charley's brown bread. I have to record with shame that after the fall of that sheep I became much less pious than I had been before ; and yet, on the whole, my sufferings in this subterranean prison, and the marvellous and

—including Charley's vision—miraculous ways in which my life had been preserved, and by which I was restored safe to the upper world, gave such a serious turn to my thoughts and manner of life that, though frequently assailed from without and from within by infidel reasonings and suggestions, I have never since then doubted the existence and omnipresence of an over-ruling Providence.

CHAPTER XXX.

MY LAST ATTEMPT UPON THE SEALS' TUNNEL.

BECOMING now heartily tired of that niche-cutting labour I determined to make a fresh attempt on the Seals' Tunnel On the last occasion I had failed, but at that time I was living upon a fish diet. My food now was fish, roast mutton, and wholesome brown bread. I was far stronger, and should certainly be able to penetrate several yards farther into the tunnel which led from that second blow-hole into the sea.

I had very carefully preserved as much of that touch cloth as was not necessary for the lighting of my second fire. Now, again, taking it as before in my purse, and securely fastening the latter with whip-cord till it was quite water-tight, I dived through the first reach of the tunnel. Not to be tedious here, especially as my attempt was frustrated, let me say that I

lit my fire as before, and made several most
determined attempts to penetrate the tunnel
beyond the second blow-hole—the little one
three yards in diameter. I learned now exactly
at what point of time my power of retaining
breath was half exhausted. I kept on diving
and groping along the tunnel till I had reached
that point of endurance, and then returned. As
I became acquainted with the nature of the
tunnel, I found myself at each fresh attempt
able to travel further.

All my efforts, however, were fruitless. Save
that second small blow-hole I could not find
another. Finally I determined to give up for
good all thoughts of making my escape by the
tunnel, and to devote my energies to the slow,
but in the end sure, method of cutting footsteps
in the incline at Curry's Window. Before,
however, finally betaking myself to the great
cavern, and renewing my labours at the window,
I made a complete exploration of this minor one
which opened off the first blow-hole.

Here, now, I lit a great many fires, and

explored it in every part, hoping that I might there meet with something that might be of service to me. At last, in a remote corner which I had not quite illuminated formerly, I discovered a beam of timber of considerable size. I notched it with my knife. All the outer part was quite soft and crumbling, but as I went on cutting I discovered, to my joy, that the inside was quite hard and sound. I saw at once that a more rapid means of escape lay before me. I could cut this beam into small blocks, convey the blocks through the tunnel, and pile them up at Curry's Window. Had I made a proper exploration of this minor cavern when I was here before, I might have been at home now. I returned home, dined joyously, and smoked my tobacco down to within two inches of the end of my coil of Limerick twist.

I have mentioned before that I knew a good deal of poetry by heart, and that the repetition of what I knew was a great comfort to me during the whole time of my imprisonment, and prevented my mind from preying on itself.

This night I repeated the whole of the first three books of "Paradise Lost," which I had committed to memory when a school-boy. I had, indeed, a good deal of difficulty with those passages in which the chief persons in Satan's host are identified with the gods of the Gentile natives in and around Palestine, but eventually got all correct.

I believe I did not go to sleep till near morning, and when I did at last fall asleep, slept an unconscionably long time. When I awoke it was late in the afternoon of the next day. Without waiting for breakfast I dived through the tunnel, and coming up in the minor cavern found that my fire, though carefully covered up with ashes, had gone out. This was a great blow to me, for the mahogany from which I hoped to cut pieces was in a remote part of the cavern, and I feared to venture towards it in the dark. I might lose my way there, and although in the long run I might find my way back to the water, yet it was quite possible that while groping round there in the

dense darkness my fire in the great cavern might
go out. Indeed, I was somewhat divided in my
mind already as to whether it was my best plan
to stick to the mahogany or to my work of
stair-cutting. Now, at all events, I determined,
as I had no light by which to work at the great
beam of mahogany, to betake myself to the big
cavern and the neighbourhood of my own fire,
and work steadily at the stairs in Curry's
Window. Accordingly I did so, and found
the work progressing far faster than I had
expected.

The going out of my fire in the second
cavern seriously alarmed me. The thought was
continually present in my mind that my fire
here by the Seals' Pool might go out too. This
haunting fear prevented me from sleeping
soundly. I was perpetually starting up at night
and examining the heap of ashes in which my
precious brands were embedded to see if they
were alive. Impelled by this fear I now became
a chandler, and succeeded in making some extraordinary candles. When I afterwards showed

one of them to my mother, I thought she would never cease laughing.

A bowl-shaped depression in the floor of the cavern near the pool served me for a pot. In this I rendered the fat of the sheep, having first heated the rock with fire. In the meantime I made wicks of twisted sheep's-wool. Very thick and clumsy wicks they were, but quite good enough for me. When I had a dozen of these ready I commenced to make my candles. I drew each wick through the little pool of liquid tallow, and then hung it to dry between two boulders, suspended from a piece of timber laid cross-wise.

This labour gave me more amusement and satisfaction than anyone can realise. At home we used to make our own supply of candles. Once every year there was a great candle-making day. Then the big coach-house was cleared out, huge quantities of tallow rendered in great cauldrons there, and hundreds of "dips" made and stored up for the year's consumption. This was always a great day for

us while we were children, and looked forward
to as a most joyful event. My mother always
presided over this operation. Indeed, in all
respects she was a good housekeeper, and as like
the lady described by King Solomon as anyone
I have ever met anywhere.

In short, I made a good store of candles,
each almost as thick as my wrist in the middle,
but at the lower end bulging out to the size of a
turnip. After this when I went to sleep I used
to light one of my candles, and thenceforth was
able to pay proper attention to my slumbers,
which I could not before, owing to the manner
in which my dreaming thoughts continually
revolved round the idea of the extinction of my
precious fire.

One day—I considered it the 2nd but
it was really the 3rd of December, for I had
missed one day during that season of exhaustion
and apathy—I was returning to my work after
dinner, a meal of which I regularly partook at
three o'clock, which, however unfashionable, was
our dinner-hour at home. I was whistling

lustily, and had just turned the angle of rock where the cavern after going parallel with the coast curved towards the entrance, when I saw in Curry's Window, between me and the sky, a slight, boyish, long-legged figure. At the very moment that I perceived it, this figure shouted or screamed, "Jack." I as quickly shouted "Ned," and also as loud as I could roar, "Stop, stop, stay back"; but I might as well have shouted to a madman.

In exactly the same manner as I had done, he first pushed himself eagerly along the incline, then he slid with no power to check himself, then came rushing down the steeper portion of the slope, and at last tumbled into the heap of sea-weed which I had piled there.

Had he seen me at any distance beneath him, he would at once have suspected the nature and depth of the incline, and remembered that I was a prisoner there against my will. But my voice came to his ears as from one standing almost on the same level with himself. In starting from the foot of the incline, boulders stood up higher and higher as one passed into the interior. So he did not suspect the existence of the great depth which separated him from the ground below the incline.

In this manner Ned too was trapped, and the cavern held two prisoners instead of one.

CHAPTER XXXI.

EDWARD FREEMAN'S NARRATIVE (*continued*)—

LIFE OF THE TWO BROTHERS IN THE CAVERN.

NEXT morning, in fine spirits, we both rose early, and after breakfast commenced rolling such boulders as we could set in motion in the direction of Curry's Window. We worked hard till dinner, and went at the work again shortly afterwards, not deserting it till we were hardly able to stir from fatigue. At supper Jack said, "I fear, Ned, that our task is a bigger one than I anticipated. We have now got to Curry's Window nearly all the boulders that you and I together can remove." I pooh-poohed Jack's low-spirited view of the situation. I was so delighted with the novelty of everything, I could not even for a moment harbour such thoughts. That we two could not, almost as soon as we chose, climb out at Curry's Window, or in some other way escape triumphant out of

R

our prison, I utterly refused to believe. If it were not for the sorrow of our people at home, which I knew must be great and heart-breaking, I would have been as happy as anyone could be. It was all so like what might be read in a famous boys' story-book, and yet it was all true. Here we were both immured in our vast cavern, amid strange echoes, reverberations—in a huge darkness, faintly lit by the light of our fire, with our seals, like Elijah's ravens, bringing us food. It was all so strange and interesting. At first I was obliged to keep well out of view of the seals, who, after the first alarm, gradually became accustomed to my presence, though it was several days before I ventured to show myself, and it was then only by slow degrees that I could get them to tolerate me. They were very susceptible to music. I saw from their motions that they liked my whistling best. Jack was displeased at this—or I thought he was—so forebore, and took every opportunity of alluding to the extraordinary affection which subsisted between them. At the end of the second day we had shifted a good many pebbles to Curry's Window; yet the top of the heap was still a great distance from the window. We could not pile one stone on the top of another, owing to their smoothness and roundness. The base of this pile had to be made broad, so we were obliged to use for the pediment many of our precious stones. Of our two fishing-rods, of the bones of the sheep, and the scanty bits of sound timber found in the cave, we proposed now to make a ladder, but soon dismissed that notion. The ladder would have been much too short for our purpose, as we found after a very careful calculation.

"I fear you are right, Jack," I said at last, one evening as we sat ruminating by the fire. "To-morrow we must begin cutting steps in the rock. It is too bad to think that all your labour was thrown away."

(Those first steps that Jack cut were now useless, being covered by the boulder stones.)

"There is a better plan than that," said he. "In the lesser cavern there is one fine beam of

timber, which is quite sound when you get to
the depth of two or three inches. It is a great
deal too heavy for us to roll into the water.
But we might cut it into movable lengths and
get the pieces through the tunnel. I think
that is our plan; but it will be long and hard
work, for the beam is mahogany."

We agreed to adopt that plan, and to set to
work in the morning. I, for my own part,
made a proposition of a different kind. It was
to send out a message attached to one of the
seals. After a little consultation we hit upon a
good way of doing this. To write a letter was
easy enough. I had paper. A bit of pointed
stick, a hard fibre of seaweed, anything at all,
in fact, would do for a pen, and our own veins
would supply the ink. But how send the letter
out, attached to a seal, and at the same time
preserve it from the water and render it con-
spicuous and noticeable to anyone observing the
letter-carrier? We were not long in discovering
the right plan. Jack had carefully preserved
every portion of that unfortunate sheep which

might be put to any conceivable use. The
bones, such of them as were not still enveloped
in mutton, were in a place by themselves. The
entrails, dried and twisted, were now strong
cords. Amongst the other relics of the sheep
he had preserved the bladder. It was just the
thing for our purpose. We would put our letter
into the bladder, blow the bladder out, bind the
mouth of it firmly with twine, and attach the
bladder to our seal. So the letter would be
preserved from the action of the water, and anyone seeing our seal would see also the bladder
floating behind him when he rose to the surface.
The seal would in that case be certainly pursued
till shot. Jack, who was very sentimental—
indeed, naturally so—about his herd of seals,
did not quite like the plan, but finally consented
to the immolation of one. We selected a seal
called " No-good." He was tame enough, but
so far as Jack and myself were concerned, a bad
fisherman. In fact, he could never be taught to
bring in a fish at all, though, being young,
he was one of the liveliest of our herd. This

unproductive member of the family was selected
to be the bearer of our letter. We fastened the
bladder to one of No-good's legs, leaving a
length of about two feet of sheep-gut between
the bladder and his fin. We now dismissed
No-good, and proceeded to carry our other
purpose into execution. There was now no
necessity for repeating that toilsome operation
by which Jack had formerly kindled a fire in
his parlour, even if it were possible—for indeed
he had exhausted his materials. I had in my
pockets some lucifer matches. Two or three of
these we took and bound them up tightly in
Jack's purse. We stripped and took to the water,
Jack going first. Waiting for a few minutes
till he should be quite clear of the tunnel,
I followed—not, indeed, without unpleasant
qualms, for it was an ugly business, and though
I could swim and dive as well as my brother, I
was not at all so brave, stout-hearted, and
determined as he was. Indeed, I have never
met anyone so fearless as he. On this occasion my heart failed me, and after groping in

the tunnel for a few seconds, I came out again
as I had gone in. Then I said to myself, "If
I do not get through soon, Jack, suspecting
some accident, will return, and we may meet in
the tunnel with disastrous consequences."
Making up my mind fully to get through this
time, I dived again, and was quite surprised to
find how easy the feat really was. I came up,
of course, in dense darkness, and shouted : "All
right." I heard someone cry, "Swim this way
—I shall lend you a hand." Soon I was helped
on to the rocky shore by Jack's muscular arms,
and when we had collected some timber and had
dried our hands, we struck the matches and lit
a fire. When I for my own part had sated my
curiosity by exploring all the recesses of this
cavern, we both set to work upon the great
beam, and began to cut from it such lengths as
we thought we could roll into the water. We
found it, as Jack had predicted, very slow work.
In spite of the fire, at which we repeatedly
warmed ourselves, we soon grew cold. "This
won't do at all," Jack said. "If we are to do

a good day's work here we must swim in with our clothes on, dry them at the fire, then dress ourselves, and work comfortably." We returned as we came, dressed ourselves, dived again through the tunnel, and after drying our clothes and putting them on, worked with our knives at the beam for the rest of that day. We then covered up the embers of the fire in ashes, and diving into the water, clothes and all, returned to the big cave. That night we determined to quite shift our quarters, at least for the present, and to remove some of our food into the parlour. This we did next day, taking with us a good deal of mutton and bread. We brought through the bread easy enough by making a bag out of the sheep skin, and tying the skin up so tightly as to be quite waterproof. On the previous day we had been rather surprised to find that the seals seemed quite as fond of our society in our new quarters as in the old. There were two or three of them playing in the dark water beside us all day as we worked. Though Jack, using all his most effective gestures and phrases, con-

tinued to impress upon them that they should
get us fish, they did not do so. The new and
strange conditions and the absence, I suppose, of
Scamp from the scene, had interrupted the
association of ideas, which my brother had, with
so much trouble, succeeded in establishing in
their minds. We therefore determined to bring
Scamp in too. Jack unloosed the little fellow
for the first time. His delight was unmeasured,
and so much did he relish his freedom that
during the greater part of that day we were
unable to capture him again. Eventually we
succeeded, and had the satisfaction later on of
finding his parents bring him a fine codling,
only a small portion of which was he permitted
to devour. Of course the moment we seized
Scamp, we proceeded at once to secure him, and
compel him to make his "lodging on the cold
ground." Here, then, we continued for a long
time industriously cutting our way into the
heart of the big mahogany beam, each of us
working at his own notch. We now saw our
way clearly. This great beam of timber was

amply sufficient for our needs, but we also saw that the cutting and preparation of it would take a long time. We foresaw, too, some difficulty in getting the pieces through the flooded tunnel, but imagined we had a promising method of working out the problem.

No-good still continued to appear in the pool, with his bladder floating behind him—a comical sight, at which we often laughed. We attached, however, little importance to No-good and his mission ; we knew now that we would get out by Curry's Window, and that it was all a question of time, provided, of course, that we did not fall sick, or meet with any unforeseen accident.

It was on one of those days that that goose of a man, Mulvaney, the sub-constable, entered the cave by Curry's Window. Mulvaney, of course, thought that when he had traversed the whole cavern and shouted in every corner of it, there was no necessity for using his eyes as well as his ears. Even with his candles, had he scanned the ground attentively he should have discovered traces of us.

CHAPTER XXXII.

EDWARD FREEMAN'S NARRATIVE (*continued*)—
HOME AGAIN.

ONE morning I was awakened by a loud noise of
thumping and the swish-swash of rushing water.
I knew the significance of this. There was wild
weather abroad, and we here, though far from
the outer turmoil, were experiencing the effects.
Jack was still asleep. I got up, fed the fire with
fresh timber, and sat on the edge of the pool
contemplating the agitation .of the dark water,
and listening to the strange and horrible noises
which it made echoing in the long, high, and
winding cave behind me, the mouth of which
opened upon this pool. All our seals were here
in a row. No-good was amongst them, with his
caudal or crural ornament hanging down grace-
fully behind him, and occasionally whirled about
by the water. "We are prisoners here now,
indeed," I said to myself, for it would be

decidedly dangerous to attempt the tunnel with the water rushing through it at this rate.

After a while Jack awoke, and when we had breakfasted and played with our friends, we went again at our work. We had now thirteen good movable pieces of timber, which only needed to be cut smooth at each end, so that they might stand firmly one on the top of the other, to be ready for the escalading of Curry's Window. All that day the agitation of the water continued and grew momentarily more violent. Had we wished to do so, it would have been utterly impossible for us to traverse the tunnel. In the afternoon the monotony was interrupted somewhat by the reappearance of No-good, *minus* his appendage. The bladder was gone. That being so, we perceived how desirable it was that we should return to the big cavern as soon as possible. Our bladder might be picked up at any moment, and consequently at any moment a search party might descend into the big cavern. What would they think if they did not find us there? They would never suspect the existence of the second cave, the avenue to which was at all times flooded. It was on that very evening that Mr. Watkins and his nephews picked up our letter. As it was certain death, however, in the present condition of the water to attempt the tunnel, we quietly worked at the big beam and spent the day smoothing the ends of those pieces which we had separated. Next day we could perceive that the outer storm had evidently abated, but the agitation of our water was still too great to permit us to get through the tunnel. At last one morning when we awoke we found that the agitation had almost quite subsided. This day we resolved to bring our logs through. We rolled one of them to the water's edge, and having made it fast with the cord, gently pushed it into the water. We feared that, being waterlogged, or owing to the close grain of the timber, it might sink; in which case we intended to buoy it up by turning our sheepskin into a bladder and fastening it to the log. The log, however, swam, and our next task was to cause it to sink just sufficiently to come on a level with the mouth of that submarine tunnel, so that we might draw it through into the great cavern. This task we accomplished by tying to it small stones as sinkers. We had only succeeded in getting a few of our pieces through when we suddenly made an important discovery.

A search party had been in the cave during the time that we were weather-bound, and in our provision cranny I found the hamper of sandwiches and the flask of brandy. I recognised at once Mr. Watkins' flask. The sandwiches, some of ham and some of beef, were very welcome, though the bread was rather stale. The brandy, too—though neither of us cared in the least for strong drink—was, in our present exhausted condition, very welcome. In short, we ate, drank, and were merry that night. We sang songs, too, making the echoes ring. We certainly did not drink too much brandy and water, at least I hope not. It was the near approach of liberty which made us so festive, though, no doubt, the strong drink to which we were almost quite unaccustomed somewhat

contributed. Jack had not smoked since I
joined him. He had about an inch of Limerick
twist still left, which he often brought out and
gazed at affectionately, but did not use. He
said he was reserving it till some time when he
might really need the stimulus of tobacco. I
was a non-smoker myself then. Would that I
could say the same now! Indeed, I have a
wretched pipe in my mouth as I write these
lines.

We spent most of the next day in the
second cave cutting three additional lengths
from the beam, for we found that we had not
enough. This is the explanation of the curious
game of hide and seek which we seemed to be
playing with Mr. Watkins and his men. Mr.
Watkins was a dear good fellow, but by no
means a Sherlock Holmes.

We rose early next morning and breakfasted
in high spirits. This day we said that we
would be free. We got the rest of our pieces
through the tunnel, and rolled or carried all
of them to Curry's Window. There, on the

highest of the boulder stones which we had
already heaped, we set up one of our big
logs, making it quite firm about the base by
the insertion, and even the ramming home,
of sea-weed between the timber and the under-
lying boulders, in order to make the pediment perfectly level, hard, and secure. We had
to be cautious, for if afterwards our ladder
might happen to topple over, the fall would be
fatal. Upon the top of this first log we put a
second in such a manner that a man might step
from the first to the second. This was effected
by inserting sea-weed behind the first log,
causing it to stand out from the rocky incline to
the distance of three-quarters of a foot or so.
The base of the second log touched the rock,
but its top we caused to stand out by means of
seaweed rammed in behind it. In this way we
proposed to make our ladder, or rather our
stairs. When completed we hoped to be able to
step up to Curry's Window almost as easily as
one might go upstairs in a house. The necessity,
to which I have already referred, of making the

ends of these blocks quite smooth and level, can be now perceived. Each log had to rest evenly on the head of the one below it. When our stairs had reached a certain height Jack went up, and I handed him the smaller blocks, which he proceeded to manipulate and adjust with sea-weed in the manner which I have described. It was a little after two when our stairs were completed. Then, with a cheer which awoke a thousand rumbling echoes through the vast cavern, we hastened back to the Seal's Pool, and joyfully broiled our last dinner. Then we unloosed Scamp and bade a final farewell to all the seals. Indeed, I myself felt a sort of regret at parting with them, though my acquaintance with the gentle and affectionate creatures was so recent, but Jack fairly—— ; well it is no matter. In fine ; we bade farewell to the seals, and putting up the few things we had to bring with us, and the butt ends of our fishing rods in order to steady us in our return along the face of the cliff, ascended the stairs—congratulating each other on the excellence of our handiwork—

s

and together stood in Curry's Window, contemplating the great sea which, at the moment, was flashing in the bright December sunlight. Jack's face, though it had blenched a good deal, was now literally as bright as the sunlit sea. We made our way carefully along the little ledge. Indeed, I may as well say that *I* went carefully, for Jack, who had now been for half a year stepping about amongst the boulders of the cave, was as sure-footed as a goat. In due time we came to that yawning cleft which, ever since the days of old Curry the smuggler, had repelled men from even attempting to traverse this cliff. Jack sprang across without a moment's hesitation. It was a big leap, indeed; but the leap back was not so appalling as the leap forward, for there was plenty of foothold upon the Du-Corrig side of the chasm. As we drew nigh to Melody's cabin, that worthy, who had been released from gaol, issued huge in the little doorway, and behind him his young hopeful, that illustrious young scholar Dannie. Big Melody, who, I thought, was devoid of all amiable human

"WE STOOD IN CURRY'S WINDOW" (*p.* 274).

instincts, actually lifted up his voice and wept like a scriptural character, and the illustrious Dannie ran off to the village roaring like a little bull: " Masther Jack is found !—the two of them is found ! " All the village people and a great many of the country people, who had been celebrating the eve of the great festival in the public-house, Johnnie Melville's, if that is any matter, ran to meet us, so that it was at the head of a great procession that we reached the Rectory. Needless to say that my father, though strongly averse to such practices, made no objection when Jack proposed to send to Johnnie Melville's for a barrel of porter. It was broached on the lawn under torch-light, and there emptied. As everyone was teasing us about our place of concealment, Jack announced that he would make a speech and tell them all together about our adventures. Accordingly, as soon as he had changed his clothes—those in which he had returned were mere rags—he mounted a chair on the lawn and told them the whole story as shortly as he could. When he

s 2

had finished, my father addressed the people, and ended with a prayer, at which all the people —though, perhaps, in anything but a prayerful humour—reverently bared their heads. Most of them were Roman Catholics, but this was in the pre-Disestablishment days, when the relations between Protestant clergymen and their Roman Catholic parishioners were less strained and strange than I have been informed they are now.

CHAPTER XXXIII.

JOHN FREEMAN CONCLUDES THE STORY.—A GOOD TREASURE-TROVE AND A MORAL.

My story is nearly ended. Next day Ned and Mr. Watkins and myself descended into the Devil's Parlour. We took with us a rock-drill, blasting-powder, a fuse, and a portmanteau. The reader will probably guess our purpose. It was to break open the tomb of old Curry and appropriate his treasures. I may have had some fear of the ghost, but not enough to prevent me from rifling his tomb. We bored, charged, and blasted into fragments the big stone which debarred entrance to the little nook where his ashes lay, thereby destroying—as I have been since told—what was perhaps an important archæological relic. The fragments, however, are no doubt there

still, waiting for the Royal Irish Academy
or some other learned body to appropriate
them.

Rushing back as soon as the explosion was
over, we discovered by the light of our candles,
behind the place where the slab stood, a broken
earthen pot and a great quantity of ashes and
charred bones. Mingled with these we only
found some pieces of metal—a few of gold, but
the greater part of silver and bronze, all much
defaced and injured, seemingly by the action of
fire. But on each side of the heap of bones,
ashes, and metal-work, we found also two
smaller vases unbroken and filled, each of them
to the brim, with many rings of gold. There was
a fourth, broken too, but which evidently had
been charged in the same manner, for the rings
lay about in a heap mingled with sherds. This
crock was placed opposite the pot containing the
ashes. The rock behind these four pots had been
planed or chiselled to a flat surface, and upon
this were certain marks, but nothing in the
nature of writing—only circles, spiral lines, and

little cup-shaped hollows. All the gold and metal work we tumbled into the portmanteau, locked it, and brought up our treasures. We had come down, of course, by the cleft called the Devil's Parlour. My seals were not visible this day. Before leaving the cave on Christmas Eve I had released Scamp and given him a final kiss. How long my seals continued to haunt the cave I cannot tell. They forgot me, I daresay, sooner than I could forget them. Though it is now many years since the occurrences which I have described, I believe I would rather shoot a man than a seal.

I sold most of my treasure-trove in Dublin in the ensuing February. After giving Ned a present out of the proceeds, I had exactly £1,155 15s. over, which I straightway banked. I never finished my college course. In the following summer, yielding to the solicitations of a maternal uncle, I sailed for Australia. I am now a sheep-farmer in the county of New Hampshire, Victoria, and though I cannot say

that I have "cattle on a thousand hills," I
have many thousands of sheep on plains. My
dear brother Ned joined me in the succeeding
summer. He was doing well as a sheep-master,
but tired of the life. He is now a journalist
in Western Australia, and so far as I can judge
—for the paper which he both owns and edits
comes to me regularly—writes very well indeed.
From certain signs and tokens I believe that the
poetry which adorns it is his own. Little
Charley, though he threatened at one time to
join the Church of Rome, is now, I am glad
to say, a Low Church clergyman and rector of
the parish of Hugminton, in the shire of Essex,
and maintains manfully in those parts the sound
doctrine of salvation by faith only. With regard
to the apparition, I have to add the following.
Some of the more interesting metal-work I
showed to a college chum. He told me that
he had a friend who was well up in antiquities,
and who would be able to tell us all about
it. This friend's name was Hennessey—I for-

get his Christian name—a gentleman who, I understand, has since distinguished himself in that department of scholarship, and now occupies a position of trust under the Government.*

Mr. Hennessey referred the metal-work to some century which I forget. He said, I remember, that its characteristics were more Scandinavian than Irish, and that their partial defacement was due to the fact that they had been cast upon the funeral pyre of the person in whose tomb they were found. As I had told Mr. Hennessey nothing about how and where I found them, I was greatly struck by his penetration. Afterwards I told him the whole story of my immurement in the cavern, with the leading parts of which he was generally acquainted, for it was a common theme of conversation at the time. A pretty full account

---

* William Hennessey, a distinguished Gaelic scholar. Translator of "The Annals of Loch Cé" and of the "Annals of Ulster." Died a few years since.—ED.

had appeared not long before in the *Saunders Newsletter.* When I came to describe the personal appearance and dress of the ghost he was greatly surprised and interested, and told me that the dress was that of an antique Irish warrior. He took from a drawer a certain Irish manuscript and read out for me, translating as he went along, three or four passages in which the appearance and the costume of ancient Irish warriors was described—descriptions which quite supported his view. He said that the metal which I have described as being like gold, but brighter, was amalgam of tin, brass, and copper, a species of bronze, the secret of whose manufacture has since been lost, and that the eyes in the ghost's brooch which looked like glass, but were not so bright as glass, were probably of that substance which in Ireland is called " Kerry Diamond."

He was very much impressed by the whole of my story about the ghost, and so far from treating it lightly, was very serious indeed, and

said many times that it was "marvellous."
And marvellous indeed it was, be the explanation what it may.

When I spoke of Curry's Window he stopped me and asked whether I was sure that the fisherman had pronounced the word as I had pronounced it. "A great deal," he said, "in investigating antiquities and the significance of names depends on the exact pronunciation." I said that he had not, and that it was for convenience sake I had pronounced it so, that the fisherman had pronounced it something like "Cooree." He seemed greatly pleased and interested in this.

He told me then that this was the name of the sea-god of the southern and western Irish in the pre-Christian ages, and that in the still extant Gaelic literature there was a large variety of stories relating to this being. After the introduction and spread of Christianity in the country, the Pagan deities, he said, began to be regarded as evil beings, usually as *piasts* or great water serpents.

This seems probable, and will help to explain the singular story told to Mr. Watkins by one of the islanders, which story, as my editor informs me, he has taken from the correspondence of that gentleman and intends to publish along with my narrative.

THE END.

PRINTED BY CASSELL & COMPANY, LIMITED, LA BELLE SAUVAGE, LONDON, E.C.

Illustrated, Fine-Art, and other Volumes.

Adventure, The World of. *Cheap Edition.* Illustrated with Stirring Pictures and Eighteen Coloured Plates. In Three Vols. 5s. each.

Animals, Popular History of. By HENRY SCHERREN, F.Z.S. With 13 Coloured Plates and other Illustrations. 7s. 6d.

Architectural Drawing. By R. PHENÉ SPIERS. Illustrated. 10s. 6d.

Art, Sacred. With nearly 200 Full-page Illustrations and descriptive text. In one Vol., **9s.**

Art, The Magazine of. With Exquisite Photogravures, a Series of Full-page Plates, and hundreds of Illustrations. Yearly Vol., 21s.

Artistic Anatomy. By Prof. M. DUVAL. *Cheap Edition.* 3s. 6d.

Ballads and Songs. By WILLIAM MAKEPEACE THACKERAY. With Original Illustrations. 6s.

Barber, Charles Burton, The Works of. With Forty-one Plates and Portraits, and Introduction by HARRY FURNISS. *Cheap Edition.* 7s. 6d.

Berry, D.D., Rev. C. A., Life of. By the Rev. J. S. DRUMMOND. With Portrait, 6s.

Birds, Our Rarer British: Their Nests, Eggs, and Breeding Haunts. By R. KEARTON, F.Z.S With about 70 Illustrations from Photographs by CHERRY KEARTON 7s. 6d.

Bitter Heritage, A. By J. BLOUNDELLE-BURTON. **6s.**

Britain's Roll of Glory; or, The Victoria Cross, its Heroes, and their Valour. By D. H. PARRY. Illus. *Cheap Edition.* 3s. 6d.

British Ballads. With 300 Original Illustrations. *Cheap Edition.* Two Vols. in One. Cloth, 7s. 6d.

British Battles on Land and Sea. By JAMES GRANT. With about 800 Illustrations. *Cheap Edition.* In Four Vols., **3s. 6d. each.**

Building World. Half-Yearly Volumes, 4s. 6d. each.

Butterflies and Moths, European. With 61 Coloured Plates. 35s.

Canaries and Cage-Birds, The Illustrated Book of. With 56 Facsimile Coloured Plates, 35s. Half-morocco, £2 5s.

Cassell's Magazine. Half-Yearly Vol., 5s.; or Yearly Vol., 8s.

Cathedrals, Abbeys, and Churches of England and Wales. Descriptive, Historical, Pictorial. *Popular Edition.* Two Vols. 12s. the set.

Chums, The Illustrated Paper for Boys. Yearly Volume, 8s.

Cities of the World. Four Vols. Illustrated. 7s. 6d. each.

Civil Service, Guide to Employment in the. Entirely New Edition. Paper, 1s. Cloth, 1s. 6d.

Clinical Manuals for Practitioners and Students of Medicine. A List of Volumes forwarded post free on application to the Publishers.

Clyde, Cassell's Pictorial Guide to the. With Coloured Plates, Map and other Illustrations. 6d.

Colour. By Prof. A. H. CHURCH. With Coloured Plates. 3s. 6d.

Conning Tower, In a; or, How I Took H.M.S. "Majestic" into Action. By H. O. ARNOLD-FORSTER, M.P. *Cheap Edition.* Illd. 5d.

Garden of Swords, The. By MAX PEMBERTON. *Illustrated Edition.* 6s.

Gladstone, William Ewart, The Life of. Edited by Sir WEMYSS REID. Illustrated. 7s. 6d. *Superior Edition,* in Two Vols., 9s.

Gleanings from Popular Authors. Illustd. *Cheap Edition.* 3s. 6d.

Guests of Mine Host. By MARIAN BOWER. 6s.

Gun and its Development, The. By W. W. GREENER. With 500 Illustrations. *Entirely New Edition.* 10s. 6d.

Gun-Room Ditty Box, A. By G. STEWART BOWLES. With a preface by Rear-Admiral LORD CHARLES BERESFORD, M.P. 2s.

Heavens, The Story of the. By Sir ROBERT BALL, LL.D. With Coloured Plates. *Popular Edition.* 10s. 6d.

Heroes of Britain in Peace and War. With 300 Original Illustrations. *Cheap Edition.* Complete in One Vol. 3s. 6d.

History, A Foot-Note to. Eight Years of Trouble in Samoa. By ROBERT LOUIS STEVENSON. 6s.

Houghton, Lord: The Life, Letters, and Friendships of Richard Monckton Milnes, First Lord Houghton. By Sir WEMYSS REID. In Two Vols., with Two Portraits. 32s.

Hygiene and Public Health. By B. ARTHUR WHITELEGGE, M.D. 2s. 6d.

India, Cassell's History of. In One Vol. *Cheap Edition.* Ill'd. 7s. 6d.

In Royal Purple. By WILLIAM PIGOTT. 6s.

Jenetha's Venture. By Colonel HARCOURT. 6s.

Kilogram; The Coming of the, or, The Battle of the Standards. By H. O. ARNOLD FORSTER, M.P. Illustrated. *Cheap Edition.* 6d.

King Solomon's Mines. By H. RIDER HAGGARD. Illustrated. 3s. 6d. *People's Edition,* 6d.

King's Hussar, A. By H. COMPTON. 3s. 6d.

Ladies' Physician, The. By A LONDON PHYSICIAN. 3s. 6d.

Letts's Diaries and other Time-saving Publications published exclusively by CASSELL & COMPANY. (*A list free on application.*)

Library Year-Book. A Record of General Library Progress and Work. Edited by THOMAS GREENWOOD. Illustrated. 2s. 6d.

Little Huguenot, The. By MAX PEMBERTON. *New Edition,* 1s. 6d.

Little Novice, The. By ALIX KING. 6s.

London, Greater. Two Vols. With about 400 Illustrations. *Cheap Edition,* 4s. 6d. each.

London, Old and New. Six Vols. With about 1,200 Illustrations and Maps. *Cheap Edition,* 4s. 6d. each.

London, Cassell's Guide to. Illus. *New Edition.* 6d. Cloth, 1s.

Manchester, Old and New. By WILLIAM ARTHUR SHAW, M.A. With Original Illustrations. Three Vols. 31s. 6d.

Medicine, Manuals for Students of. (*A List forwarded post free.*)

Music, Illustrated History of. By EMIL NAUMANN. Edited by the Rev. Sir F. A. GORE OUSELEY, Bart. Illustrated. Two Vols. 31s. 6d.

Modern Europe, A History of. By C. A. FYFFE, M.A. *Cheap Edition,* 10s. 6d. Library Edition. Illustrated. 3 Vols. 7s. 6d. each.

National Gallery, The. Edited by Sir E. J. POYNTER, P.R.A. Illustrating every Picture in the National Gallery. To be completed in Three Vols. £7 7s. the set, net.

National Library, Cassell's. 3d. and 6d. List post free on application.

Natural History, Cassell's Concise. By E. PERCEVAL WRIGHT M.A., M.D., F.L.S. With several Hundred Illustrations. 7s. 6d.

Natural History, Cassell's. *Cheap Edition.* With about 2,000 Illustrations. In Three Double Vols. 6s. each.

Nature and a Camera, With. By RICHARD KEARTON, F.Z.S. With Frontispiece, and 180 Pictures from Photographs. 21s.

Nature's Wonder Workers. By KATE R. LOVELL. Illustrated 2s. 6d.

New Zealand, Pictorial. Illustrated. 6s.

Novels, Popular. Extra crown 8vo, cloth, 6s. each.

Roxane. By LOUIS CRESWICKE.
The Ship of Stars. By Q (A. T QUILLER-COUCH).
A Bitter Heritage. By J. BLOUNDELLE-BURTON.
The Little Novice. by ALIX KING.
In Royal Purple. By WILLIAM PIGOTT.
Jenetha's Venture. By COLONEL HARCOURT.
The Guests of Mine Host. By MARIAN BOWER.
The Garden of Swords. ⎫
Kronstadt. ⎬ By MAX PEMBERTON.
A Puritan's Wife. ⎭
The Sea Hoack; or, At Sea in the 'Sixties. By ALEC J. BOYD.
The Refiner's Fire. By Mrs. ERNEST HOCKLIFFE.
Potsherds. By Mrs. HENRY BIRCHENOUGH.
Some Persons Unknown. ⎫
Young Blood ⎬ By E. W. HORNUNG.
My Lord Duke. ⎭
Spectre Gold. By HEADON HILL.
The Girl at Cobhurst.
The Vizier of the Two-Horned Alexander. By FRANK STOCKTON.
Sentimental Tommy. ⎫ By J. M. BARRIE.
The Little Minister. ⎭
Grace O'Malley: Princess and Pirate. By ROBERT MACHRAY.
A Limited Success. By SARAH PITT
The Wrothams of Wrotham Court. By FRANCES HEATH FRESH-
    FIELD.
The Master of Ballantrae. ⎫
Treasure Island. ⎪
The Black Arrow. ⎪   By
Kidnapped. ⎬ ROBERT LOUIS STEVENSON.
Catriona. ⎪ Also a *Popular Edition*, 3s. 6d.
The Wrecker. By R. L. STEVENSON ⎭   each.
    and LLOYD OSBOURNE.
Ill-gotten Gold. By W. G. TARBET.

Optics. By Professors GALBRAITH and HAUGHTON. *Entirely New and Enlarged Edition.* Illustrated. 2s. 6d.

Our Own Country. With 1,200 Illustrations. *Cheap Edition.* Three Double Vols. 5s. each.

Painting, Practical Guides to. With Coloured Plates :—
    CHINA PAINTING, 5s. ; ELEMENTARY FLOWER PAINTING, 3s. ; NEUTRAL TINT, 5s. ; SEPIA, in Two Vols., 3s. each ; FLOWERS, AND HOW TO PAINT THEM, 5s. ; A MANUAL OF OIL PAINTING, 2s. 6d. ; A COURSE OF PAINTING IN WATER COLOURS, 5s.

Paris, Cassell's Illustrated Guide to. Paper, 6d. ; cloth, 1s.

Peel, Sir R. By LORD ROSEBERY. 2s. 6d.

Penny Magazine, The New. With about 650 Illustrations. In Quarterly Volumes. 2s. 6d. each.

Peoples of the World, The. By Dr. ROBERT BROWN. In Six Vols. Illustrated. 7s. 6d. each.

Peril and Patriotism. True Tales of Heroic Deeds and Startling Adventures. In Two Vols. 4s. each. Also in One Vol., 7s. 6d.

Phrase and Fable, Dr. Brewer's Dictionary of. *New and Enlarged Edition.* 10s. 6d. Also in half-morocco, Two Vols., 15s.

Picturesque America. In 4 Vols., with 48 Steel Plates and 800 Wood Engravings. £12 12s. the set. *Popular Edition,* 18s. each.

Picturesque Canada. With 600 Original Illustrations. Two Vols. £9 9s. the Set.

Picturesque Europe. POPULAR EDITION. In **Five** Vols. Each containing 1½ Litho Plates, and nearly 200 Illustrations. 18s. each. *Cheap Edition.* (The British Isles). Two Vols. In One. 10s. 6d.

Picturesque Mediterranean, The. With Magnificent Original Illustrations by the leading Artists of the Day. Complete in Two Vols. £2 2s. each.

Pigeons, Fulton's Book of. Edited by LEWIS WRIGHT. Revised, Enlarged, and Supplemented by the Rev. W. F. LUMLEY. With 50 full-page Illustrations. *Popular Edition,* 10s. 6d. Original Edition, with 50 Coloured Plates and Numerous Wood-Engravings. 21s.

Planet, The Story of Our. By Prof. BONNEY, F.R.S. With Coloured Plates and Maps and about 100 Illustrations. *Cheap Edition.* 7s. 6d.

Playfair, Lyon. Memoirs and Correspondence of Lyon Playfair, First Lord Playfair of St. Andrews. By Sir WEMYSS REID. With Two Portraits. 21s.

Poultry, The Book of. By LEWIS WRIGHT. *Popular Edition.* 10s. 6d.

Poultry, The Illustrated Book of. By LEWIS WRIGHT. With Fifty Coloured Plates. *New Edition in Preparation.*

Poultry Keeper, The Practical. By LEWIS WRIGHT. With Eight Coloured Plates and numerous Illustrations in Text. *New and Enlarged Edition.* 3s. 6d.

Q's Works, Uniform Edition of. 5s. each.
> Dead Man's Rock. Also *People's Edition,* 6d. The Splendid Spur. The Blue Pavilions. The Astonishing History of Troy Town. "I Saw Three Ships," and other Winter's Tales. Noughts and Crosses. The Delectable Duchy. Wandering Heath.

Queen's Empire, The. Containing nearly 700 splendid full-page Illustrations. Complete in Two Vols. 9s. each.

Queen's London, The. Containing nearly 400 Exquisite Views of London and its Environs, together with a fine series of Pictures of the Queen's Diamond Jubilee Procession. Enlarged Edition. 10s. 6d.

Rabbit-Keeper, The Practical. By CUNICULUS, assisted by Eminent Fanciers. With Illustrations. 3s. 6d.

Railway Guides, Official Illustrated. With Illustrations, Maps, &c. Price 1s. each; or in cloth, 1s. 6d. each.
> LONDON AND NORTH WESTERN RAILWAY, GREAT WESTERN RAILWAY, MIDLAND RAILWAY, GREAT NORTHERN RAILWAY, GREAT EASTERN RAILWAY, LONDON AND SOUTH WESTERN RAILWAY, LONDON, BRIGHTON AND SOUTH COAST RAILWAY, SOUTH EASTERN AND CHATHAM RAILWAY. Abridged and Popular Editions of the above Guides, paper covers, 3d. each.

Rivers of Great Britain: Descriptive, Historical, Pictorial.
> RIVERS OF THE SOUTH AND WEST COASTS. 42s.
> THE ROYAL RIVER: The Thames, from Source to Sea. 16s.
> RIVERS OF THE EAST COAST. *Popular Edition,* 16s.

Robinson Crusoe, Cassell's **Fine-Art** Edition. *Cheap Edition.* 3s. 6d. or 5s.

Roxane. By Louis Creswicke. Ex. crown 8vo, cloth, 6s.

Royal Academy Pictures. In One Vol. 7s. 6d.

Ruskin, John : A Sketch of His Life, His Work, and His Opinions, with Personal Reminiscences. By M. H. Spielmann. 5s.

Russo-Turkish War, Cassell's **History** of. With about 500 Illustrations. *New Edition.* Two Vols., 9s. each.

Saturday Journal, Cassell's. Yearly Volume, cloth, 7s. 6d.

Science Series, The Century. Consisting of Biographies of Eminent Scientific Men of the present Century. Edited by Sir Henry Roscoe, D.C.L., F.R.S. Crown 8vo, 3s. 6d. each.

    John Dalton and the Rise of Modern Chemistry. By Sir Henry E. Roscoe, F.R.S.

    Major Rennell, F.R.S., and the Rise of English Geography. By Sir Clements R. Markham, C.B., F.R.S.

    Justus Von Liebig: His Life and Work. By W. A. Shenstone, F.I.C.

    The Herschels and Modern Astronomy. By Miss Agnes M. Clerke.

    Charles Lyell and Modern Geology. By Professor T. G. Bonney, F.R.S.

    J. Clerk Maxwell and Modern Physics. By R. T. Glazebrook, F.R.S.

    Humphry Davy, Poet and Philosopher. By T. E. Thorpe, F.R.S.

    Charles Darwin and the Theory of Natural Selection. By Edward B. Poulton, M.A., F.R.S.

    Pasteur. By Percy Frankland, Ph.D. (Würzburg), B.Sc. (Lond.), and Mrs. Percy Frankland.

    Michael Faraday: His Life and Work. **By Professor** Silvanus P. Thompson, F.R.S. 5s.

Science for All. Edited by Dr. Robert Brown. *Cheap Edition.* In Five Vols. 3s. 6d. each.

Sea, The Story of the. Edited by Q. Illustrated. In Two Vols. 9s. each. Cheap Edition. 5s. each.

Shaftesbury, The Seventh Earl of, K.G., The **Life and Work** of. By Edwin Hodder. *Cheap Edition.* 3s. 6d.

Shakespeare, The Plays of. Edited by Professor Henry Morley. Complete in Thirteen Vols., cloth, 21s. ; also 39 Vols., cloth, in box, 21s. ; half-morocco, cloth sides, 42s.

Shakespeare, The England of. *New Edition.* By E. Goadby. With Full-page Illustrations. 2s. 6d.

Shakspere, The Leopold. With 400 Illustrations. *Cheap Edition.* 3s. 6d. Cloth gilt, gilt edges, 5s. ; roxburgh, 7s. 6d.

Shakspere, The Royal. With 50 Full-page Illustrations. Complete in Three Vols. 3s. 6d. each.

Ship of Stars, The. By Q (A. T. Quiller-Couch). 6s.

Sights and Scenes in Oxford City and University. With 100 Illustrations after Original Photographs. In One Vol. 21s. net.

Social England. A Record of the Progress of the People. By various Writers. Edited by H. D. Traill, D.C.L. (Completion.) Vols. I., II. & III., 15s. each. Vols. IV. & V., 17s. each. Vol. VI., 18s.

Sports and Pastimes, Cassell's Complete Book of. *Cheap Edition.* With more than 900 Illustrations. Medium 8vo, 992 pages, cloth, 3s. 6d.

Star-Land. By Sir Robert Ball, LL.D. Illustrated. *New and Enlarged Edition*, entirely reset, 7s. 6d.

Sun, The Story of the. By Sir ROBERT BALL, LL.D. With Eight Coloured Plates and other Illustrations. *Cheap Edition.* 10s. 6d.

Technical Instruction. A Series of Practical Volumes. Edited by P. N. HASLUCK. Illustrated. 2s. each.
    Vol. I. Practical Staircase Joinery
    Vol. II. Practical Metal Plate Work.
        (Other Volumes in Preparation.)

Tidal Thames, The. By GRANT ALLEN. With India Proof Impressions of Twenty magnificent Full-page Photogravure Plates, and with many other Illustrations in the Text after Original Drawings by W. L. WYLLIE, A.R.A. *New Edition*, cloth, 42s. net.

Treasure Island. By R. L. STEVENSON. *Illustrated Edition.* **6s.**

"Unicode": the Universal Telegraphic Phrase Book. *Desk or Pocket Edition.* 2s. 6d.

Universal History, Cassell's Illustrated. Four Vols. 9s. each. *Cheap Edition,* 5s. each.

Vicat Cole, R.A., The Life and Paintings of. Illus. In 3 Vols. £3 3s.

Wars of the 'Nineties, The. A History of the Warfare of the last Ten Years of the 19th Century. Profusely Illustrated. In One Vol. 7s. 6d.

Westminster Abbey, Annals of. By E. T. BRADLEY (Mrs. A. MURRAY SMITH). Illustrated. *Cheap Edition,* 21s.

Wild Birds, Familiar. By W. SWAYSLAND. Four Series. With 40 Coloured Plates in each. (Sold in sets only; price on application.)

Wild Flowers, Familiar. By Prof. F. EDWARD HULME, F.L.S., F.S.A. With 240 Beautiful Coloured Plates. *Cheap Edition.* In Six Vols. 3s. 6d. each.

Wild Life at Home: How to Study and Photograph It. By RICHARD KEARTON, F.Z.S. Illustrated from Photographs by CHERRY KEARTON. 6s.

Wit and Humour, Cassell's New World of. 2 Vols. 6s. each.

Work. The Illustrated Weekly Journal for Mechanics. Half-Yearly Vols. 4s. 6d. each.

"Work" Handbooks. Practical Manuals prepared *under the direction of* PAUL N. HASLUCK, Editor of *Work.* Illustrated. 1s. each.

World of Wonders. Illus. *Cheap Edition.* **Two** Vols. 4s. 6d. each.

ILLUSTRATED MAGAZINES.

The Quiver. Monthly, 6d.

Cassell's Magazine. Monthly, 6d.

The New Penny Magazine. Weekly, 1d.; Monthly, 6d.

"Little Folks" Magazine. Monthly, 6d.

Tiny Tots. For the Very Little Ones. Monthly, 1d.

The Magazine of Art. Monthly, 1s. 4d.

Cassell's Saturday Journal. Weekly, 1d.; Monthly, 6d.

"Chums." The Paper for Boys. Weekly, 1d.; Monthly, 6d.

Work. Weekly, 1d.; Monthly, 6d.

Building World. Weekly, 1d.; Monthly, 6d.

The Gardener. Weekly, 1d.

Sunday Chimes. The Illustrated Magazine for the Day of Rest. *New Series.* Weekly, 1d.; Monthly, 6d.

CASSELL & COMPANY, LIMITED, *Ludgate Hill, London.*

Bibles and Religious Works.

Bible Biographies. Illustrated. 1s. 6d. each.
The Story of Moses and Joshua. By the Rev. J TELFORD.
The Story of the Judges. By the Rev. J. WYCLIFFE GEDGE
The Story of Samuel and Saul. By the Rev. D. C. TOVEY
The Story of David. By the Rev. J. WILD.
The Story of Joseph. Its Lessons for To-day. By the Rev. GEORGE BAINTON.

The Story of Jesus. In Verse. By J. R. MACDUFF, D.D.

Bible Dictionary, Cassell's Concise. By the Rev. ROBERT HUNTER, LL.D. *Illustrated.* 7s. 6d.

Bible Student in the British Museum, The. By the Rev. J. G. KITCHIN, M.A. *New and Revised Edition.* 1s 4d.

Bunyan, Cassell's Illustrated. With 200 Original Illustrations. *Cheap Edition.* 3s. 6d.

Child's Bible, The. With 200 Illustrations. *150th Thousand.* 7s. 6d.

Child's Life of Christ, The. With 200 Illustrations. 7s. 6d.

Church of England, The. A History for the People. By the Very Rev. H. D. M. SPENCE, D.D., Dean of Gloucester. Illustrated. **Complete** in Four Vols. 6s. each.

Church Reform in Spain and Portugal. By the Rev. H. E. NOYES, D.D. Illustrated. 2s. 6d.

Doré Bible. With 200 Full-page Illustrations by GUSTAVE DORÉ. *Popular Edition.* 15s.

Early Days of Christianity, The. By the **Very Rev. Dean** FARRAR, D.D., F.R.S. LIBRARY EDITION. Two Vols., **24s.**; morocco, £2 2s. POPULAR EDITION. Complete in One Volume; cloth, gilt edges, 7s. 6d.; tree-calf, 15s. *Cheap Edition.* Cloth gilt, 3s. 6d.

Family Prayer-Book, The. Edited by Rev. Canon **GARRETT**, M.A., and Rev. S. MARTIN. With Full-page Illustrations. **7s. 6d.**

Gleanings after Harvest. Studies and Sketches by the Rev. JOHN R. VERNON, M.A. Illustrated. *Cheap Edition.* 3s. 6d.

"Graven in the Rock." By the Rev. Dr. SAMUEL KINNS, F.R.A.S. Illustrated. *Library Edition.* Two Vols., 15s.

"Heart Chords." A Series of Works by Eminent Divines. 1s. each.

MY COMFORT IN SORROW. By HUGH MACMILLAN, D.D.

MY BIBLE. By the Right Rev. W. BOYD CARPENTER, Bishop of Ripon.

MY FATHER. By the Right Rev. ASHTON OXENDEN, late Bishop of Montreal.

MY WORK FOR GOD. By the Right Rev. Bishop COTTERILL.

MY ASPIRATIONS. By the Rev. G MATHESON, D.D.

MY EMOTIONAL LIFE. By the **Rev.** Preb. CHADWICK, D.D.

MY BODY. By the Rev. Prof. W. G. BLAIKIE, D.D.

MY GROWTH IN DIVINE LIFE. By the Rev. Preb. REYNOLDS, M.A.

MY SOUL. By the Rev. P. B. POWER, M.A.

MY HEREAFTER. By the Very Rev. Dean BICKERSTETH.

MY AIDS TO THE DIVINE LIFE. By the Very Rev. Dean BOYLE.

MY SOURCES OF STRENGTH. By the Rev. E. E. JENKINS, M.A., Secretary of Wesleyan Missionary Society.

Helps to Belief. A Series of **Helpful** Manuals on the Religious Difficulties of the Day. **Edited by CANON** TEIGNMOUTH-SHORE. Cloth, 1s. each.

MIRACLES. By the Rev. Brownlow Maitland, M.A.

THE ATONEMENT. By William Connor Magee, D.D., late Archbishop of York.

Holy Land and the Bible. A Book of Scripture Illustrations gathered in Palestine. By the Rev. CUNNINGHAM GEIKIE, D.D. CHEAP EDITION. 7s. 6d. .SUPERIOR EDITION. With 24 Plates. Cloth gilt, gilt edges, 10s. 6d.

Life of Christ, The. By the Very Rev. Dean FARRAR. CHEAP EDITION. With 16 Full-page Plates. 3s. 6d. LIBRARY EDITION. Two Vols. Cloth, 24s.; morocco, 42s. LARGE TYPE ILLUSTRATED EDITION. Cloth, 7s. 6d. ; cloth, full gilt, gilt edges, 10s. 6d. POPULAR EDITION. With 16 Full page Plates. 7s. 6d.

Matin and Vesper Bells. Earlier and Later Collected Poems (Chiefly Sacred). By J. R. MACDUFF, D.D. Two Vols. 7s. 6d. the set.

Methodism, Side Lights on the Conflicts of. During the Second Quarter of the Nineteenth Century, 1827-1852. From the Notes of the late Rev. JOSEPH FOWLER of the Debates of the Wesleyan Conference. Cloth, 8s. *Popular Edition.* Unabridged. Cloth, 3s. 6d.

Moses and Geology ; or, The Harmony of the Bible with Science. By the Rev. SAMUEL KINNS, Ph.D., F.R.A.S. Illus. 10s. 6d.

Commentary for English Readers. Edited by Bishop ELLICOTT. With Contributions by eminent Scholars and Divines :—

    New Testament. *Popular Edition.* Unabridged. **Three Vols. 5s.** each.

    Old Testament. *Popular Edition.* Unabridged. **Five Vols., 5s.** each.

New Testament Commentary. Edited by Bishop ELLICOTT. Handy Volume Edition, suitable for school and general use. Thirteen Vols. from 2s. 6d. to 3s. 6d.

Old Testament Commentary. Edited by Bishop ELLICOTT. Handy Volume Edition, suitable for school and general use. Genesis, 3s. 6d. Exodus, 3s. Leviticus, 3s. Numbers, 2s. 6d. Deuteronomy, 2s. 6d.

Plain Introductions to the Books of the Old Testament. Edited by Bishop ELLICOTT. 3s. 6d.

Plain Introductions to the Books of the New Testament. Edited by Bishop ELLICOTT. 3s. 6d.

Protestantism, The History of. By the Rev. J. A. WYLIE, LL.D. Containing upwards of 600 Original Illustrations. *Cheap Edition.* Three Vols. 3s. 6d. each.

Quiver Yearly Volume, The. With about 900 Original Illns. 7s. 6d.

St. Paul, The Life and Work of. By the Very Rev. Dean FARRAR. CHEAP EDITION. With 16 Full-page Plates, 3s. 6d. ; CHEAP ILLUS-TRATED EDITION, 7s. 6d. LIBRARY EDITION. Two Vols., 24s. or 42s. ILLUSTRATED EDITION, £1 1s. or £2 2s. POPULAR EDITION. 7s. 6d.

"Six Hundred Years"; or, Historical Sketches of Eminent Men and Women who have more or less come into contact with the Abbey and Church of Holy Trinity, Minories, from 1293 to 1893. With 65 Illustrations. By the Vicar, the Rev. Dr. SAMUEL KINNS. 15s.

"Sunday," Its Origin, History, and Present Obligation. By the Ven. Archdeacon HESSEY, D.C.L. *Fifth Edition.* 7s. 6d.

Educational Works and Students' Manuals.

Alphabet, Cassell's Pictorial. 2s. and 2s. 6d.

Atlas, Cassell's Popular. Containing 24 Coloured Maps. 1s. 6d.

Blackboard Drawing. By W. E. SPARKES. Illustrated. 5s.

Book-Keeping. By THEODORE JONES. For Schools, 2s.; cloth, 3s. For the Million, 2s.; cloth, 3s. Books for Jones's System, 2s.

British Empire Map of the World. By G. R. PARKIN and J. G. BARTHOLOMEW, F.R.G.S. Mounted or Folded. 25s.

Chemistry, The Public School. By J. H. ANDERSON, M.A. 2s. 6d.

Cookery for Schools. By LIZZIE HERITAGE. 6d.

Dulce Domum. Rhymes and Songs for Children. Edited by JOHN FARMER, Editor of "Gaudeamus," &c. Old Notation and Words, 5s. N.B.—The words of the Songs in "Dulce Domum" (with the Airs both in Tonic Sol-fa and Old Notation) can be had in Two Parts, 6d. each.

England, A History of. By H. O. ARNOLD-FORSTER, M.P. Illustrated. 5s.

Euclid, Cassell's. Edited by Prof. WALLACE, M.A. 1s.

Experimental Geometry. By PAUL BERT. Illustrated. 1s. 6d.

Founders of the Empire. A Biographical Reading Book for School and Home. By PHILIP GIBBS. Illustrated. 1s. 8d. Cloth, 2s. 6d.

French-English and English-French Dictionary. 3s. 6d. or 5s.

Gaudeamus. Songs for Colleges and Schools. Edited by JOHN FARMER. 5s. Words only, paper covers, 6d.; cloth, 9d.

Geography : A Practical Method of Teaching. Vol. I., England and Wales. Vol. II , Europe. By F. H. OVERTON, F.G.S. 6d. each. Tracing Book, containing 22 leaves, 2d.

German Dictionary, Cassell's. (German-English, English-German.) *Cheap Edition.* Cloth, 3s. 6d.; half-morocco, 5s.

Hand and Eye Training. By G. RICKS, B.Sc. 2 Vols., with 16 Coloured Plates in each, 6s. each. Cards for Class Use, 5 sets, 1s. each.

Hand and **Eye Training.** By GEORGE RICKS, B.Sc., and JOSEPH VAUGHAN. Illustrated. Vol. I. Designing with Coloured Papers; Vol. II. Cardboard Work, 2s. each. Vol. III. Colour Work and Design, 3s.

Historical Cartoons, Cassell's Coloured. Size 45 in. × 35 in. 2s. each. Mounted on canvas and varnished, with rollers, 5s. each.

In Danger's Hour; or, Stout Hearts and Stirring Deeds. A Book of Adventures for School and Home. With Coloured Plates and other Illustrations. Cloth, 1s. 8d.; bevelled boards, 2s. 6d.

Latin-English and English-Latin Dictionary. 3s. 6d. and 5s.

Latin Primer, The First. By Prof. POSTGATE. 1s.

Latin Primer, The New. By Prof. J. P. POSTGATE. Crown 8vo, 2s. 6d.

Latin Prose for Lower Forms. By M. A. BAYFIELD, M.A. 2s. 6d.

Laws of Every-day Life. By H. O. ARNOLD-FORSTER, M.P. 1s. 6d.

Marlborough Books:—Arithmetic Examples, 3s. French Exercises, 3s. 6d. French Grammar, 2s. 6d. German Grammar, 3s. 6d.

Mechanics and Machine Design, Numerical Examples in Practical. By R. G. BLAINE, M.E. *Revised and Enlarged.* Illus. 2s. 6d.

Mechanics, Applied. By JOHN PERRY, M.E., D.Sc., &c. Illustd. 7s. 6d.

Metric Charts, Cassell's Approved. Two Coloured Sheets, 42 in. by 22½ in., illustrating by Designs and Explanations the Metric System. 1s. each. Mounted with Rollers, 3s. each. The two in one with Rollers, 5s. each.

Models and Common Objects, How to Draw from. By W. E. SPARKES. Illustrated. 3s.

Models, Common Objects, and Casts of Ornament, How to Shade from. By W. E. SPARKES. With 25 Plates by the Author. 3s.

Object Lessons from Nature. By Prof. L. C. MIALL, F.L.S. Fully Illustrated. *New and Enlarged Edition.* Two Vols., 1s. 6d. each.

Physiology for Schools. By A. T. SCHOFIELD, M.D., &c. Illus. Cloth, 1s. 9d. ; Three Parts, paper, 5d. each ; or cloth limp, 6d. each.

Poetry for Children, Cassell's. 6 Books, 1d. each ; in One Vol., 6d.

Popular Educator, Cassell's. With Coloured Plates and Maps, and other Illustrations. *Cheap Edition.* In 8 Vols., 3s. 6d. each. Also in 8 Vols., 5s. each.

Readers, Cassell's Classical, for School and Home. Illus. Vol. I. (for young children), 1s. 8d. ; Vol. II. (for boys and girls) 2s. 6d.

Readers, Cassell's " Belle Sauvage." An entirely New Series. Fully Illustrated. Strongly bound in cloth. (*List on application.*)

Readers, Cassell's " Higher Class." (*List on application.*)

Readers, Cassell's Readable. Illustrated. (*List on application.*)

Readers for Infant Schools, Coloured. Three Books. 4d. each.

Reader, The Citizen. By H. O. ARNOLD-FORSTER, M.P. Illustrated. 1s. 6d. Also a *Scottish Edition,* cloth, 1s. 6d.

Reader, The Temperance. By J. DENNIS HIRD. 1s. or 1s. 6d.

Readers, Geographical, Cassell's New. Illd. (*List on application.*)

Readers, The " Modern School " Geographical. (*List on application.*)

Readers, The " Modern School." Illustrated. (*List on application.*)

Reckoning, Howard's Art of. By C. FRUSHER HOWARD. Paper covers, 1s. ; cloth, 2s. *New Edition.* 5s.

Round the Empire. By G. R. PARKIN. Fully Illustrated. 1s. 6d.

Shakspere's Plays for School Use. 9 Books. Illustrated. 6d. each.

Spelling, A Complete Manual of. By J. D. MORELL, LL.D. Cloth, 1s. *Cheap Edition,* 6d.

Technical Manuals, Cassell's. Illustrated throughout. Sixteen Books from 2s. to 4s. 6d. (*List on application.*)

Technical Educator, Cassell's. With Coloured Plates and Engravings. Complete in Six Volumes. 3s. 6d. each.

Technology, Manuals of. Edited by Prof. AYRTON, F.R.S., and RICHARD WORMELL, D.Sc., M.A. Illustrated throughout. Seven Books from 3s. 6d. to 5s. (*List on application.*)

Things New and Old ; or, Stories from English History. By H. O. ARNOLD-FORSTER, M.P. Illustrated. 7 Books from 9d. to 1s. 8d.

This World of Ours. By H. O. ARNOLD-FORSTER, M.P. Illustrated. *Cheap Edition.* 2s. 6d.

Young Citizen, The ; or, Lessons in Our Laws. By H. F. LESTER, B.A. Fully Illustrated, 2s. 6d. Also issued in Two Parts under the title of " Lessons in Our Laws." 1s. 6d. each.

Books for Young People.

Master Charlie. By C. S. HARRISON and S. H. HAMER. Illustrated. Coloured boards. 1s. 6d.

The Master of the Strong Hearts. A Story of Custer's Last Rally. By E. S. BROOKS. Illustrated. 2s. 6d.

Whys and Other Whys; or, Curious Creatures and **Their** Tales. By S. H. HAMER and HARRY B. NEILSON. Paper boards, 3s. 6d. Cloth, 5s.

Notable Shipwrecks. *Revised and Enlarged Edition.* 1s. Illustrated Edition, 2s.

Two Old Ladies, Two Foolish Fairies, and a Tom Cat. The Surprising Adventures of Tuppy and Tue. A New Fairy Story. By MAGGIE BROWNE. With Four Coloured Plates and other Illustrations. 3s. 6d.

Micky Magee's Menagerie; or, Strange Animals and their Doings. By S. H. HAMER. With Eight Coloured Plates and other Illustrations by HARRY NEILSON. 1s. 6d.

The "Victoria" Painting Book for Little Folks. Illustrated. **1s.**

"Little Folks" Half-Yearly Volume. Containing 480 pages, with Six Full-page Coloured Plates, and numerous other Pictures printed in Colour. Picture Boards, 3s. 6d.; cloth gilt, gilt edges, 5s. each.

Bo-Peep. A Book for the Little Ones. With Original Stories and Verses. Illustrated with Full-page Coloured Plates, and numerous Pictures in Colour. Yearly Volume. Picture Boards, 2s. 6d.; cloth, 3s. 6d.

Beneath the Banner. Being Narratives of Noble Lives and Brave Deeds. By F. J. CROSS. Illustrated. Limp cloth, 1s. Cloth gilt, 2s.

Good Morning! Good Night! By F. J. CROSS. Illustrated. Limp cloth, 1s., or cloth boards, gilt lettered, 2s.

Merry Girls of England. By L. T. MEADE. **3s. 6d.**

Beyond the Blue Mountains. By L. T. MEADE. **5s.**

A Sunday Story-Book. By MAGGIE BROWNE. **Illustrated.** 3s. 6d.

Pleasant Work for Busy Fingers. By MAGGIE BROWNE. Illus. **2s. 6d.**

Magic at Home. By Prof. HOFFMAN. Illustrated. **Cloth gilt,** 3s. 6d.

Little Mother Bunch. By Mrs. MOLESWORTH. Illd. **2s. 6d.**

Heroes of Every-day Life. By LAURA LANE. Illustrated. **2s. 6d.**

Cheap Editions. Gilt edges, 2s. 6d. each.

The True Robinson Crusoe. Cloth gilt.	Home Chat with our Young Folks. Illustrated throughout.

Books for Young People. Illustrated. **3s. 6d.** each.

The Rebellion of Lil Carrington. By L. T. MEADE.	The King's Command: A Story for Girls. By Maggie Symington.
Under Bayard's Banner. By Henry Frith.	The Palace Beautiful. By L. T. Meade.
Told Out of School. By A. J. Daniels.	Polly: A New-Fashioned Girl. By L. T. Meade.
Red Rose and Tiger Lily. By L. T. Meade.	"Follow my Leader." By Talbot Baines Reed.
The Romance of Invention. **By** James Burnley.	A World of Girls: The Story of a School. By L. T. Meade.
*Bashful Fifteen. By L. T. Meade.	Lost Among White Africans. By David Ker.
The White House at Inch Gow. By Mrs. Pitt.	For Fortune and Glory: A Story of the Soudan War. By Lewis Hough
A Sweet Girl Graduate. By L. T. Meade.	Bob Lovell's Career. By Edward S Ellis.

* *Also published in superior binding, 5s.*

The "Cross and Crown" Series. Illustrated. 2s. 6d. each.

Freedom's Sword: A Story of the Days of Wallace and Bruce. By Annie S. Swan.

Strong to Suffer: A Story of the Jews. By E. Wynne.

No. XIII.; or, The Story of the Lost Vestal. A Tale of Early Christian Days. By Emma Marshall.

By Fire and Sword: A Story of the Huguenots. By Thomas Archer.

Adam Hepburn's Vow: A Tale of Kirk and Covenant. By Annie S. Swan.

Through Trial to Triumph. By Madeline B. Hunt.

"Golden Mottoes" Series, The. Each Book containing 208 pages, with Four full-page Original Illustrations. Crown 8vo, cloth gilt, 2s. each.

"Foremost if I Can." By Helen Atteridge.
"Honour is my Guide." By Jeanie Hering (Mrs. Adams-Acton).
"Aim at a Sure End." By Emily Searchfield.

"Wanted—a King" Series. Illustrated. 2s. 6d. each.

Robin's Ride. By Ellinor Davenport Adams.
Wanted—a King; or, How Merle set the Nursery Rhymes to Rights. By Maggie Browne.
Fairy Tales in Other Lands. By Julia Goddard.

Cassell's Picture Story Books. Each containing about Sixty Pages of Pictures and Stories, &c. 6d. each.

Little Talks.	Daisy's Story Book.	Auntie's Stories.
Bright Stars.	Dot's Story Book.	Birdie's Story Book.
Nursery Toys.	A Nest of Stories.	Little Chimer.
Pet's Posy.	Good-Night Stories.	A Sheaf of Tales.
Tiny Tales.	Chats for Small Chatterers.	Dewdrop Stories.

Illustrated Books for the Little Ones. Containing interesting Stories. All Illustrated. 9d. each.

Bright Tales & Funny Pictures.	Scrambles and Scrapes.
Merry Little Tales.	Tittle Tattle Tales.
Little Tales for Little People.	Up and Down the Garden.
Little People and Their Pets.	All Sorts of Adventures.
Tales Told for Sunday.	Wandering Ways.
Sunday Stories for Small People.	Dumb Friends.
Stories and Pictures for Sunday.	Those Golden Sands.
Bible Pictures for Boys and Girls	Little Mothers & their Children
Firelight Stories.	Our Schoolday Hours.
Sunlight and Shade.	Creatures Tame.
Rub-a-Dub Tales.	Creatures Wild.
Fine Feathers and Fluffy Fur.	

Cassell's Shilling Story Books. All Illustrated, and containing Interesting Stories.

Bunty and the Boys.
The Heir of Elmdale.
Thorns and Tangles.
The Cuckoo in the Robin's Nest.
The History of Five Little Pitchers.

Surly Bob.
The Giant's Cradle.
Shag and Doll.
The Cost of Revenge.
Clever Frank.
The Ferryman of Brill.
Harry Maxwell.

The World's Workers. A Series of New and Original Volumes. With Portraits printed on a tint as Frontispiece. 1s. each.

John Cassell. By G. Holden Pike.
Richard Cobden. By R. Gowing.
Charles Haddon Spurgeon. By G. Holden Pike.

General Gordon. By the Rev. S. A. Swaine.
Sir Henry Havelock and Colin Campbell, Lord Clyde. By E. C. Phillips.
David Livingstone. By Robert Smiles.

The Earl of Shaftesbury. By Henry Frith.
Dr. Guthrie, Father Mathew, Elihu Burritt, George Livesey. By John W. Kirton, LL.D.
George Müller and Andrew Reed. By E. R. Pitman.

Thomas A. Edison and Samuel F. B. Morse. By Dr. Denslow and J. Marsh Parker.
Sir Titus Salt and George Moore. By J. Burnley.
George and Robert Stephenson. By C. L. Mateaux.

Charles Dickens. By his Eldest Daughter.
Handel. By Eliza Clarke. [Swaine.
Turner the Artist. By the Rev. S. A.

Sarah Robinson, Agnes Weston, and Mrs. Meredith. By E. M. Tomkinson. 1s. only.
Mrs. Somerville and Mary Carpenter. By Phyllis Browne. 1s. only.

*** *The above Works can also be had Three in One Vol., cloth, gilt edges, 3s.*

Cassell's Eighteenpenny Story Books. Illustrated.

Three Wee Ulster Lassies.
Up the Ladder.
Dick's Hero; and other Stories.
The Chip Boy.
Roses from Thorns.
The Young Berringtons.
Faith's Father.

By Land and Sea.
Jeff and Leff.
"Through Flood—Through Fire"; and other Stories.
The Girl with the Golden Looks.
Stories of the Olden Time.

Gift Books for Young People. By Popular Authors. With Four Original Illustrations in each. Cloth gilt, 1s. 6d. each.

The Boy Hunters of Kentucky. By Edward S. Ellis.
Red Feather: a Tale of the American Frontier. By Edward S. Ellis.
Rhoda's Reward; or, "If Wishes were Horses."
Jack Marston's Anchor.

Frank's Life-Battle; or, The Three Friends.
Uncle William's Charges; or, The Broken Trust.
Tim Thomson's Trial. By George Weatherly.
Ruth's Life-Work. By the Rev. Joseph Johnson.